NightBook

Short Story Anthology

Courtney Barriger

Universal Language

ISBN 978-1-4675-4131-2

For all my friends and family
past, present, and future

and to those who inspire growth.

True love is the love of truth.

NightBook

Acknowledgements

I wish to thank the forces that be for forcing a near death experience on me, inspiring a mere college student to become an author. No, actually I chose my hardships... but I would like to thank God, and thank challenging, but rewarding experiences for building stories I can share with anyone who likes to indulge them.

Chapters

Lady Flight

Muse

Prima

The Bestiary

The Mural

The Pyramid

The Composer

The Process of Forgetting

Lady Labyrinth

Lady Flight

Tangled patches of palmetto entrench the dune I fight my way up. I imagine the sun is setting, but I can't be sure. Three days in the womb of the dark canopy have stripped away my sense of time. At least my compass gives me a sense of space, for the trees do not. They crowd me in; above, below and around.

As I can't see the sky through the canopy, I can only guess that it is late in the day by the fading song of the birds. A few hours ago I was followed by a curious flock of mangrove cuckoos. They chuckled and laughed to one another at the sight of the strange, awkward animal who obviously is not suited to trample through this overgrown part of the world. And once they had their fill of mocking me, they left me to ponder my current state alone again.

The thick palm fronds, ferns, low-laying oaks and pond cypresses never end! My peach-fuzz skin is bruised and lacerated from hours of struggling with brambles; knots and vines too thick for my stolen machete to clear. I gave up on using that tool a long time ago. The undergrowth is so intertwined that I am occasionally forced to hoist myself into the low hanging branches and play in the trees like on a jungle gym to move at all.

Sweat beads form salty spheres on my forehead and roll, stinging into my eyes. I lean my weight against the trunk of the twisted oak and wipe them away with a grimy hand. Nothing encouraging can be discerned through the haze of humidity. I peer in vain for a break in the growing madness that begins to engulf me. From where I perch, the canopy appears to go on forever. I heave a heavy sigh but refuse to rest. I must keep going. Brushing the orange strands of hair from my sweaty face, I trudge ahead.

Since I was a little girl, I played in the pleasant woods on the edge of my parents' homestead. The simple neighborhood of bright young pine trees and knee-high gardenia that had been my fairy playground led me to underestimate the complexity of the forest it gave way to;

the ancient wood that borders the township I used to call home. I was accustomed to exploring our property and clearing paths with the help of my four brothers. They taught me how to fell trees, chop firewood, and avoid snakes and spiders. They also showed me the boundaries of the property and warned me, "On your mother's life, do not go past this point."

But now, for the first time, I push past the limbs of gnarled trees and try my hardest to make it through the living labyrinth alone. On my mother's life, I must break through to the other side before I lose my sanity!

"When will you grow up and do something for the family?" my eldest brother asked me three days ago. "I can't believe how lazy you are." When I did not respond he continued, "I can't wait for you to see how the world really works. You need to wake up and stop messing with the junk in the drawing room and do something productive with yourself." He glanced at my parents for support, "like weed that garden you half made last spring, or, if you really wake up, you can marry the bailiff's son."

I did not even break a sentence from the leather bound book I was reading. I simply turned my head away from his direction and twirled my bare foot off the end of the tattered couch. The family sat together in the parlor - each to their own practice as usual on a week night- but the eldest of the siblings was no longer entertained by the backgammon game he was losing to his younger brother.

He grunted and stomped the floor, calling for my attention. "Hey! I'm talking to you!" Everyone looked up from their board games to see what the commotion was about. "You and everyone else in the family know that we are going to lose the farm. We are barely surviving on great-grandmother's left over money and the bailiff knows this. With the economy the way that it is, and property worth next to nothing, if you marry his son we can be active in the town again and not have to spend every night in this suffocating house." He glared at me, "your selfish pride is making the family suffer."

I swallowed rising words and kept to my book to avoid a fight.

"Father," he pleaded, "she needs to do her part for the family and marry. You know this!"

"How does the world really work then?" I demanded, ignoring his other comments.

My father spoke up. "You will have to learn that on your own," he replied glancing up from his guitar. He was a tinkerer himself though he was too shy to admit it. With a sigh, I looked toward the drawing room. He caught my thoughts and answered, "But you must learn it here in the township."

"What do you mean by that?" I said sweetly, trying my best to hide the aggravation in my voice.

"I see you staring at the antique maps on the walls every day, little one. I am not blind yet." He set the guitar next to the fireplace and met my resolute expression with a frown. "The world beyond these woods is a dark and evil place for a young girl like you. It is in your best interest to stay here where we can protect you. We don't want to see you get hurt."

Even if he meant it, it wasn't what I wanted to hear. I stood up and paced before the stone fire pit, the flames flashing in my eyes. Repetition, always repetition in this house! How do they know what is out there if they haven't left the township themselves! What is it like on the other side? It can't be as boring as it is here! The ignorance of his words pulsed through my veins and I finally said what had been on my mind for months.

"Father, our town doesn't hold anything for my future."

Each family member stopped their busy work and looked up. It was as though they saw what they had been dreading. It was the face of the sister they always knew, but with a different voice. My energy seemed to radiate from my face.

"It holds the bailiff's son," the eldest retorted looking away.

I snorted, "I don't care about him! He wears ruffled shirts and talks about money as if it were part of his manhood." Mother gasped. "I don't like being in spitting distance of pigs like him, so why would I ever marry one?"

"Because men like him can keep our family from living in a sty!"

"Uhg, I don't want money. I would rather be homeless and sleep in a tent than with a man I don't love," I threw my book onto the couch.

"Well you might just get your wish and bring the whole family down with you, you spoiled brat."

"AHHHH!" my head screamed but I fought back the well of angry tears on the verge of spilling. If I looked at him any longer, I would lose control and throw him against the wall. So I turned to my father instead.

"You and mother have trained me with a top rate education and the proper skills to survive on my own," I pleaded. "Why do that and not expect me to use it?"

"Shut up, you're stupid." the brother closest to my age looked up, glinting at me. "Do you think you deserve better than us?"

The crackling fire was the only sound in the room besides the tap of my steel tipped boot on the wooden floor. His opinion surprised me and paused my delivery; he usually agreed with my ideas. Maybe he didn't want to lose his closest friend.

But my intent was resolved. The boys always teamed up after all. And as a force, outside opinions hardly mattered. Since I had everyone's full attention, I tried to reach them all at once. I took a deep breath.

"Not better or worse. Just, different. What is right

for the group may not be right for the individual. Dad, you taught me Empiricism - to learn from experience - that is what I want to do." I spun around to face my sock-darning mother, "Mom, your grandmother left the very moment she was of age! Went into the forest alone with nothing but her desire to explore. She did it all! Made her own wealth and came back with a husband, six kids! We owe everything we have to her!"

The eldest brother opened his mouth, "No," I stopped him with my hand. "I will not listen to you! *She* is who we should listen to!" I pointed to the leather journal I had thrown on the floor, "because she made us what we are. And her thoughts are still with us!"

Grabbing the book from the ground, I flipped it open to the page I was reading before they could interrupt. "She said that the only thing that keeps people in place is fear." In black cursive, almost too faded to read, the passage near the beginning of the book was circled and underlined by the writer. To the family I read:

"…for years it kept me silent. It kept my mouth sealed tight so as not to disrupt the order of life. Afraid to say this place doesn't fill me. Afraid of things I don't know and how I will change once I know them. I want to conquer fear itself. Fear is what holds me back from knowing!

I pace the public greenhouse again today with the hope of finding a love to take me away from here. Maybe I will fall in love with nature and the forest will embrace me. Or maybe a trader who can take me north, around the old forest. If neither happen, I will go anyway.

<blockquote>
Moving, moving, with nowhere to go
I live in a cage, this much I know
So go, leave, wander and never come back
To the life you would squander;
filling not what you lack
</blockquote>

Eyes, bright eyes that watch as I ponder
Their quiet encouragement makes me feel stronger
They pause as they pass
When they smile, I laugh
And the sun stays bright just a little bit longer.

Green and brown
Leaves on the ground
This garden is nicer when no one's around.
In the quiet I focus
In the chorus of locusts
I find what I sought without making a sound."

Pausing from reading, I focused on each one of them. They could all recite great-grandmother's poems. But I knew they hadn't emphasized the tiny notes at the bottom of the page as I had. Beneath the poem, a few sentences were scrawled in faded ink. "The fear of the unknown is undone by spontaneity," I read. "It will take an act of spontaneity for me to find what it is I lack."

It was as though great-grandmother's voice spoke through me. My voice rang with truth and my family was rendered speechless by the power of her words through my lips. Lightheaded and dizzy, I slowly closed her journal and waited for someone to ruin the moment with an idiotic comment.

Instead, they stared at my tall, still figure unsure of what to do. I had never expressed my opinion so bluntly before. In this family, the youngest keep their thoughts to themselves and do what they are told. I had never dared to break that mold.

"Humph," the eldest responded.

"Wait, I don't get it," the middle son replied, "so you want to leave to find love or you want to leave to find gold?" Everyone looked at him.

"She wants to shirk her responsibilities and live in a fantasy in the drawing room," the eldest cut me off before I could provide an answer.

"What! I -"

"No you idiot," the youngest son snorted, "She just wants to get away from us because she thinks she is better than us. She thinks she can live up to the legend of great-grandmother and come back all glamorous to show us up."

They nodded heads at each other and grunted in agreement. "Absolute foolishness. She will get herself killed." They crossed their arms together.

"Face it sis," the youngest grinned leaning back in his chair, "you are staying here with us."

"You don't have the money or the transportation to leave the township anyway." The middle son added reasonably. With that they turned back to their games having lost interest in my challenge. I gritted my teeth at their lack of imagination.

"Darling," my father spoke softly, trying to bring me back to reality, "it takes over a month for the most experienced traders to navigate north through the passage of the Anterondak Mountains before they can head east for the harbor. There is no other way through the mountain range besides that route; and it is extremely expensive and dangerous.

"You aren't listening!" I cried over him, "I know the passage through the Anterondaks is not suitable! I would follow great-grandmother's..."

"Great-grandma was a quack who made up stories to make her dull life seem interesting," the youngest butt in again. "She probably hid out by herself for a few years and then robbed a few traders on their way back from the sea; took their gold, and convinced one of them to marry her...probably with drugs...who knows what she really did?" My jaw dropped with indignation.

"No one is alive who can account for it," he

8

continued, "There is no way to prove any of it. Manure, I tell you. All of it."

"What are you talking about?" I gaped at him, "How did you get to be so bitter?"

"Look sis," the eldest interjected, "bottom line is, just forget it. Every person who set foot past the township boundaries in the past decade never made it back to tell about it; so don't even consider that an option. You have arrangements to fulfill. Let marriage meet your need."

"Yes darling," my father agreed, "and maybe plant another garden," and went back to playing guitar.

I ran away that night. After hours of arguing with myself while watching the moon rise over the sleeping town, I reached my resolution. In the quiet midnight I rose from my bed and tread softly over the wood paneled floor, carefully avoiding the creaky loose board by my dresser. Under a flickering candle I took my book bag off its hook and opened it.

Opening my closet, I chose a knitted sweater my mother made for me, a light-weight gardening skirt, a pair of slacks, two pairs of clean socks and some undergarments. Throwing them into the bag, I tucked my boots under my arm and tiptoed out of my room and down the long hallway toward the kitchen. From the cupboards I grabbed a bag of mixed nuts, carrots, dried beef jerky and a special honey my mother collects from the hives on the property that she calls honey nectar. I filled two canteens with water from the sink. That should be enough to get me to the harbor, I was sure.

With one last place to go, I ventured back into the hallway. Passing by my parent's door, I paused. I placed my hand on the door and whispered love and farewell to them with a promise that I would return someday. My heart rose in my chest and my sight started to swim, so I moved away before emotion could change my mind.

9

Stepping onto the thick carpet in the drawing room, the smell of old books and antiques greeted me for the last time. With great care I took my great grandmother's old machete from its mantle over the fire place and held it in my trembling hands. The weight was light and comforting, and the handle easy to grip. The metal was slightly rusted, but the blade was still sharp and as it slid it into the bag I shivered at the prospect of using it to protect myself.

From the roll-top desk I pocketed an old compass. Bypassing the useless faded maps, I took the only thing of value in our house - my great-grandmother's famous journal - and quietly slipped out the front door and into the thick humidity of the night.

The village was in a deep summer sleep. Only a single light could be seen shining down from the full moon. It lit the dark green hills that tapered down to my home and reflected off of the rushing brook that bordered the lilac meadows by the bailiff's manor. The town itself was a hazy shadow tucked into a wide bend on the river's southern shore.

I made my way up into the hills of my family's land with a heavy but determined heart. The property held a score of small grassy downs that sloped up to the north to become a finger of the Anterondak Mountains; to the east they diminish into the edge of the old forest and continue on to become craggy, tree-lined cliffs and bramble-filled burrows in the depths of the wood.

At the edge of the tallest down, I pulled the hood back and took one final look at the shaded, single story homestead resting in the distance. It seemed as though it were inside a snow globe; as if time was in slow motion only there and no place else. The wind caught the trees and leaves fell so gently over the front porch.

"Goodbye," I whispered to my house. "Goodbye," I whispered to sleepyville. With a sense of peace I turned my back on all I knew. I stood then on the threshold of a tall hill, my boots in the mist, and ahead the broken hills rolled down into the gathering darkness that is the tree-line of the old forest. Clouds gathered in boughs of the shapeless trees before me. The old forest stretched on into infinity and I knew the moment I stepped under their realm they would not let me out until I reached the border on the far east.

Moonlight illuminated the first of the giants with an unearthly glow. Further in, between the trunks I could distinguish nothing but the purest ink black. Those silent giants have been there since before I was born and will be there until I die. They whispered my name softly through the wind ever since my January birth eighteen years ago. They have been waiting for me to come to them. And as their high branches tossed in the breeze, I couldn't ignore their invitation any longer.

I broke into a sprint and plunged down the last of the hills into the first battlement. With gentle sighs and cracks they welcomed me into their labyrinth. There were no cleared paths to follow so I made my own. I listened to the music of the trees; the rushing of the leaves above and the crunch of dead twigs underfoot. Behind, the last twinkling moonlight disappeared between the trunks: and then I was truly alone.

A bolt of excitement zipped through my veins despite the danger, and I dashed like an orange dart, whooping and hollering down the slopes. I danced like a sprite, twirling beneath the twined branches; I was no longer a daughter, no longer a sister, no longer a citizen, pupil, or congregant. I was a spirit of the wood and laughed at myself for ever being afraid at all.

The landscape flew by in a haze. Deep in my prefrontal cerebral cortex, neuropathways were zooming and connecting every abstract thought my head had ever cooked up; and with the help of adrenaline, I reached new levels of consciousness with every step.

The undergrowth began to thicken as I ran. I leapt over tree roots and giggled as I dashed between trunks. And as I passed near a small brook I planted a foot into a mossy hole and flew forward onto my face. Coughing, slightly winded on the ground, I spat up dirt, brushed off my scraped hands and elbows and muttered, "Uhg, I need to pay attention to where I am going!"

True enough, I did need to pay attention, because the sky was brightening, and I had the feeling that it was too soon to be sunrise. Could I have run for four hours? Must have. From what I read in the journal, it takes five days to cross the forest - and that is only if you have enough sense to travel in a straight line, which is hard to do in the canopy.

Suddenly exhaustion came over me like a warm blanket. Still on the ground, I fixed my long hair into a bun, flipped over onto my back and lay down. My bed was the thick mossy soil; my book bag was my pillow. The treetops swayed lightly and through them, the sky began to show the light blues of the coming dawn. The last stars were barely visible through the branches. Listening to the leaves rustle, I fell asleep dreaming of chasing the sun.

That morning was three days ago, and I have since then come to discover that the wild wasn't coined such for no reason. The wood isn't "wild" in the sense that isn't domesticated like our family mule; The wild is in every way unruly, uncontrollable and in the most realistic sense, barbaric. My pink tailored clothes are stained black with sweat and grime; arms and legs, once unblemished as a fresh peach, are now marked with bruises, scabs, and scrapes. I have eaten most of my food out of sincere exhaustion, and have only a few sips of water left in the canteen. But still, no matter how famished I become while enclosed here, I have enough knowledge of the wood to know not to consume anything that grows wild. There have been enough cases of berry and mushroom poisoning in our hounds at home for me to know not to touch them, even in the most desperate of circumstances.

Since that first dawn when I chased Helios in his great chariot, I have not seen even a glimpse of blue through the twisting trunks. The days and nights are almost indiscernible. Endless layers of thick leaves up above cast me in a world of impenetrable shades of black and grey. The tree trunks seem to glow white in the darkness, and the air is quiet and still aside from the rustlings of a few small squirrels. Yet somehow, the summer heat reaches my pores and my sweat soaks through the back of the light pink sleeveless top I poorly selected from my dresser drawer the night I left.

Since I awoke, an hour's hike in has lead me to an unavoidable and nearly impassable undergrowth. I plodded in with no alternative. The plant life grows almost on top of each other, and a few feet in I lost all standing space. Over time, the space between the trees gradually became tighter and tighter until I found myself crawling underneath the thicket, through mud and thorns, finding rest only by laying prostrate in dank puddles.

So I crouch, hunchbacked, with aching limbs and joints, climbing through the endless maze of low hanging branches, shrubbery, and pricklies with the hope of finding a clearing or a large enough space for me to stretch my back.

For the past three hours, an unfamiliar patch of fern growth infesting the roots in this region has drenched the air with pungent oils, making each breath a struggle. It fogs my focus, limiting my concentration to the uncomfortable stickiness of my throat. Even with a handkerchief tied around my mouth, I wheeze and cough with the failure to expand my lungs enough to get oxygen to all of my parts. It triples my exhaustion and dehydration. I lick my lips, pause to pick a shiny sweet gum leaf from its branch and pop it in my mouth, breaking apart the leaf with my front teeth to suck on the flavor. Hopefully the tartness will excite my salivation glands so I can swallow property.

With a sigh I shake my head to try to wake up. Either I am so tired that my waking life has become a lucid dream and I am completely imagining things, or that elephant-sized tree trunk really did just shift two feet to the right - far enough to completely block the opening between the two mangroves I was going to take.

Come on! It has taken four hours to navigate this route, it can't end here! Perhaps it was foolish to go through rather than around this patch, but I swear, five seconds ago, there was enough space for me to do a summersault between the gaps of those trees, and now I can barely fit a fist through.

Seriously, what is going on? I fancy the plants are conspiring against me! This isn't the first time I've noticed dramatic shift in the forest just as I am about to make a pass. It is as if the moment I blink my eyes or rest my head in the mud, they move to block the way through. I am coming to believe that the trees in this part of the wood aren't friendly at all.

They must see me as an enemy! I don't think they have seen anything like me before. Maybe they don't know what I am so they try to block me in to study me - they are grouped rather close together and seem to silently watch and pass judgment as I try to make my way among them. But who are they to try to know what I am or what I am doing? Who are they to pass judgment! So what if I am strange in this part of the world, if they were in mine they would be stranger!

They lean in closer and whisper dark threats to my sanity. I slap my face a few times and look around. I can't go forward because the huge mangrove tree is in the way; and the thick thorn bush I just climbed through seems to have grown since I last looked. I can't go back either! I am stuck!

Breathe, just breathe, I tell myself. You are calm, you are relaxed. Do not panic.

The air feels like it's thickening and I have to lean against the trunk of a cypress to catch my breath. But as I try to relax I get the sense that they are breathing too; breathing oxygen, not carbon dioxide; taking the very substance out of the air. How can this be?

"What? I- What do you want from me?" I say aloud in desperation. "Why won't you let me through?"

I feel movement in the bark beneath my hand and the old, crumbling cypress seems to stir. It cackles that I am young - just a sprout - too young with too small a root system to grow tall enough to reach the light. *It will never survive*, it tells the others.

My hand recoils from its trunk. "What! No!"

And look at how weak the limbs are the mighty oak bellows with its knurled branches around me, *it can barely support that one object, how will it hold the weight of many? It is weak.*

"But I-" I can only whisper in response, my book bag growing heavier with each thought.

It has no thorns, says the thorn bush, *it will be beaten quickly with no way to fight back.*

And it is so gullible! Says the giant mangrove gleefully, *look how easy it was to lead it into our grasp.*

My eyes grow wide.

Worst of all, the patch of putrid ferns notes solemnly, *it is completely alone. It has no support. If it falls then that is it! The last of its kind is gone.*

The blood in my veins boiling, I clinch my fists and straighten my back up as much as I can.

"STOP!" I find my voice, "Stop, stop, stop!" echoes off their trunks. "Let me be!" The way back is barred by the thorn bush. I spin in a circle, holding my head. "Stop this! Let me through!" I plead to the mangrove, "There are more of my kind where I am going! I am just passing by!"

The trees laugh as I struggle to squeeze between the mangrove and the silent birch wood. "Please!" I cry to them, "I am - I am just another creature, like you! Only, only different."

This thing is nothing like us, says the cypress to the mangrove; *do not move till we know what it is.* The mangrove agrees with its elder and holds its place. I turn to the cypress.

"Look!" I spread my fingers wide and twirl them around in circles, "I have roots! And look here," I extend my arms and legs as far as I can. "I have branches too! Branches strong enough to carry my weight and whatever else I choose to take to the top; to the light. Though for that," addressing the oak, "I would need your help because you're right, I will never be tall enough to see it on my own."

The trees are silent in thought, so I turn to the thorn bush. "And, I have weapons," my voice lowers, "though only one of them is a thorn." I slowly unsheathe the machete and the trees seem to pull away from its presence. I brush the blade among the ferns, and they quiver. The space around me feels lighter.

"But you see," I examine the thin branches of the thorn bush, and it seems to shake without the wind, "I have no need to use this here. I am not going back in that direction." Turning to the two trees blocking the way I run my hand down the bark of the birch. The birch and the mangrove do not even budge. Even with this tool, I am not able to get through their barrier to where I need to be.

"Uhg," I sigh, still unable to move. This is a ridiculous predicament. I slowly close my eyes and rest my heavy head on my knee. The trees shake and whisper to each other about my physical make up, but their words are lost in swirling thought. I do not care anymore. I do not care about anything. They can think and say whatever they want, it doesn't change the fact that they are just a group of trees; five of trillions in this wood and I happened to be trapped in by the most judgmental of their kind.

There are so many of them and only one of me. It all seems so unfair, but then again, I was the one who set out from home by myself without really knowing what to expect. If only they would get out of my way! It isn't like I am bothering them on purpose; it causes unrest because they can't figure me out. But I were to explain myself, they wouldn't listen or understand or accept. I know it.

But the trees and I really are the same thing. We are all organic matter, living and breathing: dependant on this decaying planet to survive. They just happened to be cast as seeds here in this forest where they are fated to fight each other for the duration of their lives to make it to the sunlight. The Cypress was right; we are all trying to get to the light.

The ground rumbles and overhead the branches of the birch wood begin to untwine from the twisted mangrove tree. Its' roots inch up from the ground like worms, and scoots its body, grumbling and rumbling, two feet over to the right; creating a hole just large enough for my tiny body to fit through.

I crouch to my feet, smacking my head on an oak limb, then, quick as lightning I lunge for the pass between the trees before anything can stop me. As I scrape against the birch I hear it say.

It is a vine. And the others mumble in agreement.

Suddenly my heart leaps into my chest. A hundred yards ahead, past the choking fern patch and brick-stacked trees I see a radiant, green glow emanating through the leaves. It stands out like a brilliant white spot on a black panther. I am immediately like a moth, unhindered in my desire to enter that light. Breathe, I tell myself, breathe. In quick, frantic bounds I shove past the roots and shrubbery with my eyes trained on the oasis. My face is scratched by trees' fingernails. My orange hair is ripped and torn leaving strings the forest floor. Almost there.

Finally, I snap apart the last few branches and collapse into the streaming sunlight. My body feels like a beaten sack of potatoes that has been battered and bruised on the back of a careless trader. Lying spread eagle and broken on the moss padded ground, taking in the fresh air and the warm sunlight of the small circle clearing, I relax every muscle and gaze thankfully at the open sky. Freedom from the brambles! There is no hurry move for a while. No rush. There is time to spare.

With a light sigh I close my eyes and listen to the movement of the wood with open ears. Strange. There is no wind so there are no sounds from the trees. But even stranger, I can't hear any animals. I strain my ears to locate any life other than mega flora, but I cannot sense any warm-blooded mammals, reptiles or even insects in the area.

The sky begins to fade out and my eyes grow heavy. My body feels light as air, smooth as water. In the quiet, I take the plunge into the pool of the dream world. The cold swirling depths strip my senses of perception. It sweeps me into a whirling vortex of cushioned liquid. I spin around, a mass of color, unhindered with no place to touch ground. Swaths of black pulse beneath pressured eye lids, quick, faint flashes of light that make my body twitch and writhe, and still, a sense of purity bathes me in frigid waves until my body curls into a ball and holds itself to feel whole again. Heart beat moves in great swells, warmth spreads to every limb and I unfold again with grace.

Through the pulsing, lucid water, a new vibration is picked up. It tingles my ears, sending new pulses down my body. The melody agrees with me. It sounds like a crystal glass singing; so natural, so harmonious. Something in it says *listen with your heart and you hear everything.*

18

The gentle progression of chords breaks the bubble of my sleep and I rise in mystified confusion. The sun has dipped out of the opening in the canopy leaving me in the shade again. I nod my head to the side as if my ears will leak water and once again they pick up a twanging note. The song is real! I listen harder - the melody falls then rises, calling me to my feet. I forget my stubbed toes and am drawn to the edge of the clearing.

But wait! This beautiful song is being played by a person! My eyes flash at the realization. I am not alone after all! Someone else is traveling through the old forest just as I am. Whoever it is must be crazy to call attention to them in a dangerous place like this. What are they doing? A silly smile drifts across my face. I must meet this musician. There is something about this song and this place that connects me to this composer.

In a foggy haze I follow the music to the Northern edge of the clearing and duck my head to enter the wild again.

NightBook

Courtney Barriger

Muse

The current heaves white water into the jetty of jagged rocks, and its churning waves destroy the quiet solitude he came for. With weary hands he grasps his guitar and holds it close, away from the force of the salty wind. Its strings are muted by the gale, maybe he alone can hear it; yet he plays it with as much gusto as he would when performing for a full venue. The battered cherry-wood guitar, given to him as a writ of accomplishment from a mentor long forgotten, is now his only reliable companion; everyone else left and moved on, leaving him to question his intentions again.

A sad, sweet melody is picked by this musician's finger tips that rise and fall with each warm breath. Staccato threads are plucked externally to sever the part of his heart he is forcing to die today. He remembers the last words she said to him, the day she walked away last summer, a year ago.

Their relationship was deep, blood thicker than water; and the both were sweet. He can't forget all the talks they had, and the walks; and the conversations that sometimes made each other mad. Now on this rock he laughs looking back on that, because even in those times they never had it that bad.

Recalling what that brunette said last, he sings the one phrase aloud to the sea, "Listen with your heart and you hear everything." The anthem carries across the turbulent water and disappears as if it is received by the ocean herself; odd that the brunette's suggestion hurt him. He should know how to listen with his heart since composing with his heart is his life's purpose. If only his heart wasn't always divided…

Ten years of attempting to influence the growth of humankind through his music forced him into isolation again. He writes to resolve the division between the positive realm and the negative realm within oneself. But the black and white becomes shades of grey, and often leads his actions to be misinterpreted. His desire for ultimate unity leaves him conflicted and abandoned. But still, he continues to live his philosophy, as long as he is able to confess his struggles on the summer shore to the Gods of Nature.

His somber, blue eyes sweep the horizon. The sharp smell in the wind promises a downpour soon. Under his breath, he whispers a desperate request for a crack in the fortress of clouds - for a break from this expanding shadow of self-loathing. But in the heavens above, thunderclouds gather at the forefront and sunlight cannot make it through the battlements.

He didn't mean to hurt her, but she didn't understand him. Her game was so predictable. She was just an obsession last summer made to fill the time. The deepening gloom seeps inside him and awakens decades of painful memories in his mind's eye; moments so tremendous in number he sinks lower in their onslaught.

Sea spray dampens his heavy heart and he cries:

"I stand amid the roar
of a surf tormented shore
And I hold within my hand,
grains of the golden sand.
How few! Yet how they creep
through my fingers to the deep,
While I weep- while I weep!"

He recalls Edgar Allan Poe's words with joyful spite. What timeless emotions are expressed in poetry! Written word. How universal is the suffering of the human condition!

"God! can I not grasp
them with a tighter clasp?
God! can I not save one

from the pitiless wave?"

The inlet answers with a gust of chilly northern wind that stirs the slumbering gulls from their perches. It swirls and cackles around him. The stronger the wind becomes, the more his muscles tighten. His heart aches for change but he does not know what to change. With mounting agitation he pulls his brown hair from his eyes.

"This is all so pointless!" He shouts into the wind, "So pointless! It makes me want to cause damage. Not because I delight in seeing harm done, but I need to feel real. I study every shred of evidence that convinces me that I am a figment of my own imagination.

I want to love someone so badly, and feel love in return. Isn't that the greatest thing? Love might make this real. Death might make this real too."

Not caring if anyone hears, his dichotomies pour out; "If only we knew the mysteries of time and memory, this might seem real. I feel like I am going to explode or implode. My happiness comes and goes. My emotions are never constant. One minute I worry obsessively, the next minute I am as calm as the eye of a storm.

Existence drives me insane! There are too many books to read in one lifetime. There are too many ways something can actualize. Possibilities are endless, yet I am dealing with the greatest tug-o-war a soul can survive. I think of suicide every day, and imagine myself leaping from the roof plunging eight stories down. I kill myself smoking these cigarettes. I envision grabbing the gun in the violin case and seeing what is after death. Months seem like years. One more night without meaning and I will cause damage!"

He jumps to his feet and fills the cove with a strangled yell. He screams and screams until he feels his anger purge away. As his heart rate falls, he takes a deep breath and exhales a long, compelling hum from the core of his being. His mantra transforms into a simple song that he carries into the evening air. Its' resonance pierces the darkness and the raging cove begins to slow its' pace. The surging waves pause their argument to listen.

He sings of a deep longing for spiritual connection; to hear with his heart; for love and hate to get along; for vision. In a cry he asks the ocean to attract money, success, inspiration, and beauty to him. His voice climbs higher and stronger in his spell, and soon even the gulls forget their struggles and began to chime in the chorus. It feels like years of caged tension are finally released.

The lapping water changes to playful splashing, he stops singing. Ears strained, he focuses on the new noise. *Now that isn't natural*! He inches closer to the edge of the rock; few yards down, in a soft vortex between the rocks, an orange mass swirls beneath the surface of the green swells. Smoky spirals in coils appear and disappear in the froth of the wave. He shakes his head in wonderment. *What is this vision?*

Clouds obscure the sun and the water turns murky again. "Screw this weather!" He places the guitar in a nook on the rock and makes his way down for a better view. At the water's edge, he leans over and searches for a sign of the apparition.

Glimmering sparkles like sequins on a gown glint from the depths below. He opens his eyes wider and tries to peer through the wavering light. The shimmers vanish underneath the indistinguishable orange swirling mass. Try as he might, he cannot make out a solid shape through the dark water. He lies on his chest, squinting through sea spray as he tries to focus.

Above, the weather Gods become interested. One by one, they call back their knights; the cloud band retreats and the wind, quieting her banter, blows an encouraging breeze to cool the air. The inlet is filled with warm light and the open sky illuminates the plants in a rainbow of fresh colors.

      With a new wave of confidence, the man shakes off his boots, rolls up his trousers, and nimbly treads into the basin. Stopping where he judges the thing to be, he snatches a handful of white pebbles from the rubble around him and begins dropping them, one-by-one, into the depths beyond the edge of the rocks. A satisfied smirk plays his face when he catches a glimpse of orange drift from beneath the ledge in the pool. It looks like an immense, jellyfish - colorful and iridescent. With anticipation, he watches it float up from the bottom. It seems to move against the current, as if provoked by the disruption from the stones. How strange. So he drops another one.

      He stifles a gasp. As the pebble sinks, a set of long, opal fingers shoot out from the tangerine vapor and snatch it away. The mass is alive! It is some exotic, nameless life form that keeps to the refuge of the cove. Suddenly, exposed to this monster, he loses his daring and takes a step back onto solid stone; the fist-full of rocks escaping his grasp, scattering into the water.

      Through the flurry of pebbles, the creature seeks and pin-points its assailant. In a rush it vaults through the air and lands the rocks before him.

      Braced against the jetty, he can only gape at the fantastic display before him. Arched on the rock sits the most beautiful creature he has ever seen; a tangle of glimmering orange hair frames the face of a young, porcelain woman. The ferocity her hair color against her naked, translucent skin creates an entire opal of spectrum. But what is this? Where there should be legs there is instead a long, elegant tail; wide as a whales fin, but slender like an eels, with an intricate patchwork of mirror-like scales; a sea-green garment of sequins. So stunning! So magical! She faces him defiantly, with her onyx eyes issuing a challenge.

      He raises his hands above his head illustrating

surrender, but the creature does not know human gestures. Tilting her head, her unblemished face questions his movements. He isn't sure if she is angry, curious, or a mixture of the two, so he steps a little closer just to see what she will do. In one great movement she swishes her tail and sends a wave over him, completely drenching him from head to toe.

"Whew!" He sputters, wiping his eyes, "Now just wait a minute!"

She cannot understand what he said, but his messy reaction brought out bubbling noise from her that he discerns as laughter. If laughter it was, those black eyes do not relent. She studies him with the smooth calculation of a predator. He swallows his fear, forces a smile and takes another cautious step toward her. This time she does not budge; her gaze traces the movements of his feet and then slowly makes its way up his body to rest on his eyes.

His heart beats faster. That mesmerizing face of hers is a magnet; he has no control over the pull of its force. Try as he might to look away, she has him locked in. He kneels down and places himself before her, at her mercy. She sits like a glimmering statue, perfect and immovable. Trembling, he reaches out his hands, places them on her smooth face, and caresses her cheeks. Her skin is frigid on the surface, but warm and alive beneath. Slowly, he brings his face closer to hers and in a in a rush of excitement he forgets himself and kisses her.

For a moment, nothing exists but the two of them joined together. The world spins around them. She puts more force into it, adding the soft taste of her salty tongue. Nothing in his mind can compare to this. The way she smells like the sea, the strange rhythm of her heart, the way she fits perfectly in his arms - this is the place he longed for, this unexpected place of perfection.

Then she jolts up, and with wide, surprised eyes turns and dives back into the sea, her glittering tail vanishing into the blue depths below.

Completely bedazzled, he cannot move. Gentle waves lap at his knees. Though he senses she is gone, the salty taste of her mouth lingers on his lips, and he cannot focus on anything around him. With a shock he realizes he is still at his favorite cove. The nestled gulls still sing in harmony from the crevices above, and the forgotten guitar still waits for his return. He shakes his head and blinks a few times to regain composure. What spell was this?

"Is everything we see or seem but a dream within a dream?" He asks the sky.

The Gods above smile with approval.

Courtney Barriger

Prima

On the podium that is the dance stage; I am the champion orator. With long, elegant legs, my tremendous leaps and bounds draw gasps from the captivated theater. At the purposeful flip of my wrist I can inspire tears of wonder and sighs of longing. When the song begins to fade, and I take my sumptuous bow to the floor, the audience jumps to their feet to praise my name.

My name! It lights the entire avenue before the theatre and is spoken with respect in the highest society. They marvel over my grace, my beauty, my routine. Now my routine is truly something of its' own class. Completely flawless, it has been perfected with years of careful practice and tutoring from my world renowned mentors. The Italian masters have titled me the *Prima Ballerina Assoluta,* like the great Pierina Legnani. They say that in the world of ballet, I am queen.

But I do not envision myself this way. Fame and glory have their dazzlements, true, but what brings the most satisfaction is the pristine art of the dance. Not only does it encourage the joy of moving to music, but it creates an elevated sense of physical awareness. It is like playing God: twisting and manipulating the human form for the enjoyment of a hungry crowd. "Di pui, Di pui," they shout, "More, more!" So I give them what they plead for. I use my body as a classical display of my creative mind. It becomes the potters' clay or the weavers' thread; both are just objects in the grip of an artist. With every routine, I refine my abilities and am able to move on to a higher level.

My performance tonight will be divinely unique. It is the opening for my greatest and most difficult solo act yet. In the second act of my dance I am to perform a round of 40 pirouettes before an auditorium of five thousand; that is four more rotations than has ever been done in the history of ballet! And with the careful measurement of balance and timing, I will publicly break the record of the last *Prima Ballerina Assoluta,* and prove to the world that I am undeniably superior.

Backstage I prepare for the show. As my hair is combed into a tight, orange bun and tiny white flowers are secured in the shape of crown, I play over my routine again. In rehearsal earlier I faltered on my 32nd pirouette turn twice in a row. Had it happened only once it would not bother me so much; but twice? How can I have let that happen twice? Those spins can flip your poise if you let them, but I am an expert at this point and mistakes are not acceptable. What would happen if I lose equilibrium on stage tonight, in front of a full house? How will that affect my reviews? My fans? I vehemently shake away the thought and am instantly chided by my hairdresser.

As show time approaches, I am moved to stand before a floor length mirror to approve of my appearance. The light pink corset hugs my curves and compliments my figure as it should, but feels a bit tight. No matter, look at how the fluffy tutu accentuates the length of my legs making them appear super human. Yes, I approve. They slide my slippers on, string and tie them up my ankles, dust my skin with iridescent sparkles, and dab a touch of gloss to my lips. To them, I am ready for action. To me, this is only brushing the horse before the race.

Behind the curtain, with three minutes to go, I shush my assistant as she hands me a drink and we listen to the dignified silence of the enormous crowd. She tells me that the Queen is a spectator tonight. In response I drink my entire glass of water.

Two minutes to go.

The crew disappears from the look of my glance, and my fists clench involuntarily as I force myself to relax. I have done this before…I remind myself…I have done this before. Just not this particular routine…or with this many people…or with…

One minute.

Lights begin to dim in the auditorium and the noise tapers off into silence. I close my eyes and focus all of my attention into the stance of my feet and the form of my body. Everything must be centered.

Go.

The audience gasps as the stage unveils my pale, statuesque figure; more stunning than they ever remembered. I stand in pose on the back of a great condor beneath a white willow tree. Orange and gold leaves are sprinkled from the rafters above and by the time they graze my face, the orchestra takes their cue. I rise like a morning glory to the graceful sound of the violin and tilt my head as the cello joins. At the strike of the bass drum I dash into a set of nimble chaines turns that escalade into the most stupendous attitude leap ever witnessed by the Queen in her theater. The spectators move to the edge of their seats. I extend every bound and emphasize every single chord of the symphony with my poignant poses. An appropriate sigh escapes the crowd with each stressed move and once again, the audience is my choir and I am the proficient maestro. I enter into the second half of my act with consciousness and confidence.

But what was that? I have never had this reaction from a set of sensational side leaps. It takes every fiber of self-control not to glance at my audience. I continue my routine in wondrous form but am surprised again by another startled sound from my spectators. Why are they responding to me in this fashion? This is the most brilliant I have yet performed but their feedback does not match my efforts! Dumfounded, I chance a quick glance at them as I complete a chasse. An unsettling amount of attention is aimed at something behind me off center stage. What could be causing this distraction? In my dramatic allegro pause, I look full force in the direction of the disruption.

Peeking from behind the white willow tree, I spot a brown-haired man dressed in a full fledged, red and yellow

spandex jester suite watching my dance. He marvels at me
with the same wide-eyed wonder as any fan does, yet he
possesses a certain charisma that holds my eye for a
moment too long. I stifle my anger and blink him away,
sweeping into a series of over energetic bounds. How has
this happened? How has this audacious man finagled his
way past security and onto my stage to distract my viewers
at my most important performance to date? I will not allow
him to divert any more attention.

As swift as a swooping eagle I execute my second
set of chaines turns and the crowd moans at the graceful
curve that my body takes as I transition into an arabesque.
I am coming close to the grand finale.

But what is this? Now in front of the willow the
Jester is dancing too! He appears to imitate my every move.
What nerve! Is he trying to make me falter to embarrass
my reputation or is this some amateur trick to win the favor
of the crowd? I have the urge to charge him off the stage
and leave him broken and bruised in the audience, but I
choose not to let him win my full attention. I am in my
own dance and I must complete it without him as a
distraction. So I try to forget about him as I enter the
buildups to the finale.

But what is he doing now? With purposeful strides
he speeds across the platform toward me. As his muscular
body flies into a suite of breathtaking tours, my audience is
no longer watching me at all; they are mesmerized by this
joker's astounding counter moves. Fear floods my mouth
and I swallow it back. This Jester is more competition than
I imagined.

He seems to know every pause in my routine, for
that is when he comes to life and steals the show. It is as if
he has studied my habits for ages, and though this
particular act has never been viewed by anyone but my
coach, he can already anticipate what my next feature will
be. So cunning! I am forced to play a tedious game back-

and-forth with no choice at all! As magnificent as my performance is, he mutes my award by being a great balancer.

The music slows and I take the final pause before I break into the one feat I know he cannot possibly mirror. In this moment, when I shut my eyes, relax my muscles, and tune every synapse for the great move, he skips up to me and in a bold sweep just a breath before my cue of action, he yanks off my corset and flings it to the floor.

In only a white leotard and tutu I snap into a never-ending spin cycle. From the stage I appear to be a pearlescent spinning top. They stare transfixed at this vision. Details of my appearance are swallowed in the fury of the glittering tornado. As I pull my arms closer to my solar plexus, my momentum builds. I am already at twenty - halfway there. My eyes are closed tight and I concentrate on the steadiness of the point of my toe. Without the corset I cut the air more efficiently than ever before. Twenty-five. I have more thrust at this point than I did in rehearsal. This is promising. There are not too many more spins left to go. Thirty.

Wait. How am I already losing so much speed? This doesn't feel right. Thirty-two. Each turn seems to take too long. My toes begin to blister. Thirty four. My pace is the turn of a Ferris Wheel, you can see every detail as it circles by. Thirty-five. I have hardly any energy left to finish this. My stiff leg is a battered fulcrum as I round to my thirty sixth pirouette. The crowd is on their feet. The world turns in slow motion as I drift into my thirty-seventh spin. Shouts are exclaimed and eyes are hypnotized at the dawdling completion of my thirty-eighth. I feel my body give, and as I stumble out of my thirty-ninth pirouette, the Jester rescues my tired grace and scoops me into his arms.

In a daze I hardly hear the roar of the crowd - they praise my name louder than ever before. The critics jot excited notes about my form, the women wipe away tears from the emotional duet, and the Queen ardently claps her hands at my record-breaking performance. They are clueless to the duel that was just performed before them. To them, it was part of the act! A sensational act! They chant my name in ignorance but all that I see is the knowing smile of the man who holds me high in the air like a bird in flight.

As the curtain closes and the lights dim, he places my worn feet on the ground. The awestruck crowd outside continues their naive cheers and I can only stare at this stranger in wonder. How could he interpret so much about me? My routine; he knew my routine when he couldn't possibly have…And the corset? How did he know that it was too tight for me to complete my spins? Where did this man find the daring to join me in my own dance only to salvage my ambitious pride?

His arms still around my waist, I take his hands, hold them in mine and look into his open, blue eyes. "Who are you?" I can hardly say, "What do you want from me?"

With a whimsical smile he answers, "I just want to know more about you."

The Bestiary

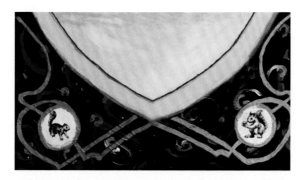

Shivering with the morning air, he snuggles his nose into her orange hair and pulls her close for warmth. This temporary home, though it serves its purpose as shelter from the nights snowstorm, does not do much to bar out the biting winter chill that slyly creeps towards them along the floor. He should have let her watch the sky during the day yesterday as she usually does, for then they might have had time to find a more comfortable place to burrow away before the storm. But the moment she tries to focus on something other than him, he feels the need to do a little dance or chirp a little tune to pull her attention back. With great care not to wake her, he untangles himself and makes his way up the dirt path into the light.

The sun begins to rise over the tops of the dense spruce trees, casting long shadows over the frost-caked under story of shrubs. Last night's snow fall was not as heavy as the past few, but still, it froze over the promising fungi growth on the tree root that he had spotted before the storm blew in. At this time of season it is lucky to find anything in the wild to munch on, especially something as fresh and plentiful as a fungi patch; the tall, thin ones are his favorite. So the famished squirrel begins to paw through the ice-crusted dead leaves for something other than compost to fill their bellies with.

A troubled squeak from the bottom of the abandoned rabbit's hole announces that his lovely new friend is awake. Her tiny white face pops out of the darkness and she blinks in the sunlight, scanning the forest floor until she spots her skinny brown mate. Shaking out the kink in her left leg, she stretches her weary muscles, yawns and then lounges her frail body on a dry patch of mulch. She watches as he continues his search, turning over a dead branch with an eye for anything crawling or squirming.

Each squirrel once had an entire winter's store of their own; the young female's bounty was especially well cared for even though she was on the move. But one too many powerful flurries sucked away their buried goods. And after a spellbinding first encounter where they found themselves cosmically attracted and inseparable, they have agreed to help each other survive these difficult times together. It has been a few days since either of them have had anything real to eat, so the search is becoming desperate.

Something smells ripe. He sniffs out the air and turns his back to her beautiful figure in pursuit of the encouraging aroma. Digging feverishly into the mush, he yanks out a shiny, black walnut shell. Skipping over to her, excited by the look on her face, he sinks his teeth into the shell and pries it apart. Inside the shell is a pool of black sludge that oozes onto his paws; like a rotten egg, the nut is repulsive, it mocks his groaning tummy. He squeaks angrily and chucks the nut and it bounces off a knotted tree root. She watches his every move in fascination and fights to hide her disappointment. He has done the best that he can to provide for them, she knows this. But there just isn't anything worth scavenging.

The sun rises higher in the atmosphere bathing their little clearing in warm light, even in their daze they appreciate the beauty of the white garden lit in glory of the sun. The first light greens shine in the dark bristled trees surrounding them, and the couple nestle into each other for warmth and comfort. Minutes turn into hours and their strength ebbs away in sync with their hope for survival.

Maybe it is time to let go. It would be such a relief to abandon the struggle here and now, and jump into the fantasy of the next life; which, of course, will be better than the one they are in now. Anything would be better than the physical and mental suffering of starving to death.

He is sick of feeling low; tired of feeling sorry for himself; of filling his time with one partner after another. Who will fill this gap? This little redhead who adores him? He feels an adoration for her innocence and beauty; so alone and unprepared for her first winter. He is loyal, wholeheartedly. With her, here, now, he could pass in peace.

She rests her head on his strength and experience. She didn't expect to fall for such an anthem as his; wild with abandonment, the opposite of her rearing. He knows the wood better than she and has a unique way of navigating it. She analyzes his judgment for comparison but trusts it more than she is aware of. A death experienced together could create a very new and unique adventure for them.

Nature can be so cruel with her timing.

A chilling breeze moves in from the south and stirs the leaves around them. With it comes a faint, shrill cry; the noise of another animal not too far away. Startled from their exhaustion, they rise to their feet and spy out their surroundings, moving as little as possible so they are not spotted. The cry was dreadfully familiar, but it was too muffled to tell what type of beast made it. The sounds of the wood are hushed by the snow. Ears pricked up, they listen for another sign without moving a muscle.

"RRAA!" echoes through a heavy patch of shrubs only a few meters away. Rumbling and deep, with a high-pitched ending, this is the cry of a hungry predator.

With the swish of a tail, the male squirrel signals for the female to follow, quickly and quietly. Almost to the edge of the underbrush, they can hear the crunch of heavy pads through the snow behind them. The stride of the beast belongs to night prowler lynx; a fierce, unforgiving consumer of the night. It must be starving mad to hunt into the morning light.

If the cat picks up their scent then it will chase them relentlessly, so the little orange one holds her breath to hide her scent as she scrambles through the bushes.

They scurry down hill; over frozen ice patches, tracking over great drifts of snow. Their movements must be inaudible as well as invisible if they hope to escape. Hearts throb in their chests, but they can take only short breaths to enable maximum speed.

As swift as they can, they leave the cover of the tall trees. The footfall of the lynx becomes distant with the growing space; it has not noticed their presence. Good. The brush tailed male sneaks them along the roots of the great spruces, and soon, he feels they are far enough away to slow their pace. They moved so fast through the broadleaved forest that they no longer recognize the landscape.

Crouched panting underneath the only brush in sight, they examine their new surroundings with apprehension. The giant trees have given out to a clearing with little vegetation; where thick snow patches litter the downward sloping ground. Further down the hill, she spots a place to hide.

In the middle of the field stands a colossal douglass fir tree - the largest living thing either of them have ever seen. It looms 250 feet in the air with its first branches crowning 65 feet off of the bristle covered ground. To the squirrels, it is the king of its kind.

They crawl beneath its massive shade and peer up

into the almost symmetrical branches. The bark is thin, gray and flaky with numerous resin blisters. Almost like cork.

An echoing growl from the recesses of the woods reaches their ears alerting them to the close proximity of the lynx. Fearful, they spring onto the trunk and shoot up the base, exerting the very last of their energy.

The ground drops further and further away as they claw higher and higher toward the safety of the branches. With tiny lungs panting, they force their arms and legs to push their growing weight onto the first of the branches, and, staggering they keep their pace until they find a large enough spot to rest. Finally, they collapse into the nook in the mass of the tree and glance down just in time to see the short tailed cat stalk by the base of the tree without even looking up.

They have evaded its attention. They are safe. Relieved but exhausted, the brush tail scoots away from the edge and looks around. They are so high above the forest floor that it would take a while for them to regain the energy to climb down; and they know they should wait as long as possible to descend, because lynxes hide out for hours until their prey reappear. But as they are unsure if they have been seen, they will wait it out anyway.

Ears twitching, he pokes around the nook of the tree to see if there is anything useful or interesting to do. It is unusual for a tree so massive to be completely isolated from the rest of its kind. And this one is the only fir tree in a forest of spruces. How did it get to be here, in the middle of a field?

And there is a strange smell in the air that he cannot place: sweet, tangy, and ripe. What is that smell? He climbs around the little olive-green shoots to try to locate the source.

The redhead notices that her friend is on the hunt, so she stands to her wobbly feet and follows the scent up the next few branches, inches her way around the bend of the trunk, and leaps over a few more to catch up with him.

As she noses around, her eyes fall on something miraculous. With a squeal of excitement, she dashes to the end of the branch where a bright green baby cone is budding out of the bark. Its sweet, sappy smell perfumes her senses and she almost faints from the intoxication. She eagerly snatches it out of its roots and scampers higher up to where she heard her mate's feet scraping around. She squeaks and squawks with the prize in her paws until he answers back from the branches above.

They run to meet each other, both brandishing green cones! Astonished with their success, they chomp into the cones together and purr with happy bellies.

But why should they stop with one cone when they could hoard an entire winter stock! This fir tree is blooming like a field of wild strawberries, and they have the luxury of finding it first.

They jump from branch to branch, pulling out as many cones as they can carry at once. But once their little arms are full, they stuff the cones into cork holes and keep moving up the tree. *On the way back down*, they assure themselves, *we will gather these again. Nothing will be wasted.*

They giggle and rub noses as they devour wild mistletoe. This is paradise. They will never be hungry again! The tree is a plentiful smorgasbord, and each level they climb offers new delicacies.

As he ascends the blissful living heaven, he leaves his mate down below. He finds a patch of the most luscious sprouts he has ever tasted, and stuffs his cheeks full of them. This is too much! Greedy handfuls of cones are collected and tossed aside at the sight of better ones. Stuffed cheeks are bulging at full capacity, so he spits everything out to fill them again.

It is so plentiful that the waste does not matter; he

tosses it all aside at the sight of the next trinket. Soon, the branches are littered with cone and sprout refuse. But he does not care one bit. He clutches at every morsel of food in sight.

A little further up, he spies the biggest, brightest bud he has seen yet. In a dash of excitement, he scampers toward the trophy and as his paws make to grab it, it is suddenly plucked from his grasp. He screeches indignantly as his female friend holds the prized cone high above her head out of his reach.

She chuckles to herself for having reached it before him.

But he is serious.

They eye each other warily.

He notices her identical sprout stuffed cheeks and scoffs at her with bristling hair and a mocking chirp.

She clutches the cone closer to her chest and when he chirps again, she spits a mouthful of chewed sprouts at his face.

He furiously brushes the junk off of him, and looks at his companion as if he just met her for the first time. She has crossed the line.

She was never docile, but she was also never any trouble. Can't she see that he is aiming high for the both of them? That they will both benefit if he brings in the resources? He just wants to take care of her. What is she doing? Why is she trying to beat him?

But before he answers his questions, in a blink he springs to the closest branch to claim the next monster cone for himself. Before *she* can.

With distaste, she notes his competition. She left the nest by herself to make a livelihood to bring back to her family, and right when she finds something promising, he has to make it into a game! She just wanted a companion. But she was doing fine in her routine before he learned it and broke it. She can take care of herself - the mangy rodent.

Her eyes fall on a cone a few branches over that are bigger than the one in her paws. She growls and throws the bud away, lunging for the larger cone.

Quick as a woodpecker pecking, he snatches it up before she reaches it, and sinks his teeth in, marking it as his property.

They growl at each other and dinner instantly becomes a fuming rat race.

Dashing ahead, he finds an unmistakable winner. Then she shows him up by finding an even better one. She admires her swiftness just long enough for him to pinch the cone from her unyielding paws and bite a chunk out of it, tossing it carelessly to the ground with a smirk of satisfaction at her socked expression.

Soon, every chosen cone has a chunk bitten from it, and from the forest floor, it appears to be snowing green shards.

They push each other, scratching and squealing over each new find, racing up the tree with no attention to the growing scarcity of cones or the thinning branches. Before they are aware, they reach the very top.

When the branches give out, they freeze in shock. A mighty ocean gust blows her off balance and she grabs his arm for support. They are at the pinnacle of the highest living thing as far as the eye can see, and the massive spruce forest below looks as minuscule as mushroom patch.

With angst, they grip the feeble sun bleached branches and search for a windbreaker so they could take better look around. And that is when they spot it.

Atop the last jut of the trunk lay a gargantuan bird's nest. The size of a small tree itself, it is made of the strangest assortment of branches and material the squirrels have ever seen.

With caution, the male signals for the frightened female to wait. He climbs up to the edge to see what it holds. The messy nest is strewn with the rotting carcasses of many different creatures; deer antlers, chunks of putrid flesh, the jaw bone of a lynx, and a few scattered squirrel tails make up the stinking pile.

Stiff with fear, he stares at the graveyard before him and pictures the size of the beast that can haul a full grown deer carcass to the top of a 250 ft fir tree. He shivers at the image.

Little red senses his fright and squeaks from the base of the nest for him to come down. Though she cannot see the massacre above her, she can feel the bad energy about the place.

It is not safe for them to be here, he realizes, they need to leave now.

As he turns his back to the slaughter, he thinks he caught sight of a faint smudge of black in the sky... almost like a moth in his peripheral vision. But it was in fact the wide wingspan of an approaching condor.

The bird wheels in circles high up in the air. With piercing eyes he scans the tops of the trees, and spotting his lair, begins his slow, graceful descent. In his blunt talons he grasps a chunk of frozen goat's leg which he carried with him from the forests of the south and has saved for an evening snack.

His northern nest is one which he visits only when he has a large meal; for this nest is his grand palace in the sky, reserved for special occasions only.

No other condor had the daring to nest so far north; in such a cold climate. But this bird is smarter and braver than his peers, and flew for weeks to find the perfect perch - higher than any other nest he has ever seen. He spent months gathering branches from the great redwoods even further north. His palace is perfect; revered among his kind.

The carcass crashes into the bone pile. With a stiff neck, he cranes his bald head around and inspects the condition of his home. Everything seems to be in place.

The prized antlers are in a neat pile as he left them, and the pig's feet have not moved from where he stocked them last week.

But wait, what is this? Something is off. On the eastern edge of nest, the wall is tattered; as if something had walked across it. And the twisted boughs below look like they have green cone heart smudges all over them.

With careful calculation, the condor examines his disturbed nest. Someone has indeed trampled through here! What creature is stupid enough to trespass on this pristine territory?

With an irate cry, he vaults into the air and swoops down on the fir tree. His keen eyes spot the chewed bits of cone and scattered mistletoe sprouts that pepper the branches… all signs that indicate intrusion by squirrels.

The sap from the buds is so fresh that the perpetrators cannot be far away.

Lower and lower he sweeps. He sees where they stashed their cones in the cork hole. So sloppy. Then he flies down to the first branches where there are shredded cones everywhere. This is embarrassing not to mention rude! Where are those tree rats? He can teach them a few lessons in housekeeping; like removing a rodent infestation.

Scanning the valley for signs of the intruders, he spies their little tracks in the snow. They aren't far…

Galloping like horses, the squirrels shoot through the reeds and grass without chancing a look back. They can hear the condor's screams echo off of the tree trunks above, and it grows closer as their scrapped paws smack the frozen ice. The undergrowth is getting thicker. Brambles tug at their fir, but they do not dare slow down.

Suddenly, a dark shadow passes overhead. The condor shrieks victoriously as he spies the two little rodents scampering below. He plunges into the thicket with open claws aimed for their tiny spines.

The squirrels sense him hovering and dive beneath

the roots of the nearest tree, tucking their bodies away into a dark corner.

Outside, the condor jabs his beak around the root system, digging his nails into the rotting wood, prying it apart with ease. With a CRACK the root snaps into pieces.

Face to face with yellow eyes, the red squirrel screeches and hisses with her hair standing on end, and as the bird's claws reach into the hole, her mate pulls her away from his piercing nails only moments before they could take her.

The male catches his mate's eye, and together, they dash to the right, beneath the bird's awkward wings, and sprint toward the familiar path they took that morning.

Wheeling around from the noise, the bird screeches and then springs into flight after them.

Up ahead, the clearing they woke up to in the morning looks brighter than they remembered. Hope fills their chests at the sight of the familiar rabbit's hole, and with reckless abandon, they run for it.

As the bird narrows his vision and prepares to dive, the squirrels take one last look at his sharp, demonic face in the sky and then lunge into the dark opening of the hole. Scampering down the alley to the belly of the cave, they pray that it is deep enough to keep out the devil.

Bodies tucked against the cold dirt wall, they hold each other and stare at the pin-point of light at the end of the tunnel with nervous dread. They look into each other's pearly, black eyes for comfort. She buries her face into his neck and shivers; and the light from outside shifts and fades all together.

Rustlings and shrieks are heard above. The cries grow louder outside, and the light grows brighter inside the rabbit hole.

Chunks of dirt fly through the air at ground level as the condor widens the mouth to try to fit in. There is nothing the squirrels can do but wait and see if their fates are doomed.

Their faces grow more distinct in the developing light. The sturdy arm of the brush-tail is the only thing that keeps her calm as death digs its steady way through the earth toward them. He nibbles her ear to let her know that he is there for her; she is not alone.

Life had been a game of survival, and when there are no more opportunities to escape, they have to allow themselves the peace to pass on to the next world. They will meet their ends together. Paw to paw, they submit to their fate.

The sounds above began to change. The pace of the black devil seems to slow and the noise of thudding dirt becomes that of scraping wood. The condor's claws met the root system of the mighty spruces. This living barrier is too strong for even the greatest bird of prey to cut through.

He pecks it with his razor sharp beak, jabs at with flying talons and throws his body against it again and again, but the roots will not give.

Panting and disheveled, the condor preens his feathers back into place and, looking off into the distance; he ponders the predicament he is in:

These rats are nearly impossible to get to, but he if keeps at it, he is bound to find a way in. At some point they will have to eat; so he could hide up in the trees till they pop their pea-brained heads out, and then swoop down and take them.

Yes, yes, what a delightful scheme!

But then again, there is a fully grown goat's leg up in the nest. It is already turning green - his favorite - and it does not require the extra effort of waiting around or exerting precious winter energy for what, an eighth a belly of food? No, no, it isn't worth it. Those pesky tree rats will probably be eaten by the neighborhood lynx anyway. With a smirk of satisfaction to cover his hurt pride, he springs up into the air and takes off and away.

Under the earth, in a meditative state, the presence of death passes over and disappears from the underground haven. Still grasping each other, they cannot move, they cannot breathe, they can not separate. Together, by their mutual acceptance of death, they connected their souls through spiritual turbulence. Like two halves meeting together to create a circle, their love is bound.

As they regain breath, the hollow feels warmer than it had before. They still cannot move but they both know they cannot stay in the safety of the rabbit's hole; they must find somewhere new, remote or they will be found out.

They must travel to find abundance. What else is out there in the dark forest? Neither of them knows what lies to the East, but there must be something better there. Anything is better. They will go together to find it, through the wood, to the edge of the world and beyond.

Courtney Barriger

The Mural

Let me paint the night sky on your ceiling,
and together, hand-and-hand,
I will lead you past the hazy layers of atmosphere
that shelter our home and our bed.

As we soar into the frigid darkness,
I pull you close for warmth.
Your rough skin electrifies mine,
and the solidity of your presence proves to me,
once again,
that my sojourns up into the unknown
cannot be accomplished without you by my side.

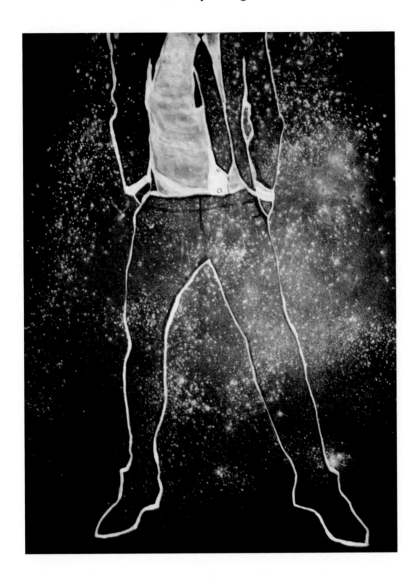

We pass the pale, dusty orb that is our planet's satellite
and say farewell to the minute sprinkle of our solar system.
Stars become a great sunset of nuances;
gaseous halos crowning the expansive heavens.
Galaxies blink by, and with great fervor
we drift far out of the boundaries of the charted universe.
This is true singularity -
suspended in this eternal void.

Together in the darkness,
I begin to see clearly the light that emanates
from the core of your being.
How beautiful!
Your radiance eats through me.
Gazing into my essence,
your voice carries your existence
far beyond the ends of the cosmos
with the simple phrase:

I Love you.

The booming resonance bounces
off of zooming asteroids that fly past us,
echoes from the twirling planets dancing by,
and bellows back to us from
the primordial super-giants.
The universe replies:

I Love you.

Those words, their meaning,
far mightier than simple human phonetics,
singe the tips of my orange hair.
Its concentration burns freckles onto my milky,
smooth epidermis and your lips start to crack
in its pervasive heat.

Aflame, our bodies become a supernova
both ancient and novel in composition.
The tumult of our whirling love-spell
illuminates the vacant paradise.
Our passion radiates in sync with billions of
constellations joined together.

In a blast of light
we shoot through the earth's atmosphere
and land back into your bed.
Ours souls are filled and satisfied
from a night spent
swimming in the fresco on your ceiling.

The Pyramid

There are silent watchers in this wide world. Beings who pass through the bustling, absent minded crowds of the city as phantoms - unseen and unnoticed by the frosted eye - until the precise moment arrives, when their advantage is the greatest and their self-assurance is strong enough to banish any doubt, they slyly begin to show themselves as what they are; and you never know what shape they will take.

With an insatiable appetite, the most powerful of these will absorb every fractal movement, every complete thought, and every unfinished dream that the village dwellers are too distracted by their mindless routines to acknowledge. She picks through each person's petty consciousness till she finds the nourishment she needs to survive her long, wasted life.

Her ability to scrutinize the trivial exchange of human interaction in her surrounding villages creates a wondrous sense of superiority. Those people are so consumed by the silly games they play that they do not notice the quagmire of negative energy it creates around them. They are blind to their own vices. The spite, jealousy, cruelty and malice that are stirred up so that one single person can get ahead generate enough hate to fuel a holocaust. In their daily interaction, they sacrifice the happiness of many for the contentment of one.

It is so simple it is almost absurd; a witch as talented as she does not need to do much to move things in her favor. What sleepwalker wouldn't follow a bright little firefly?

She laughs at how unconscious these people are. Do they know what they are doing? They would sure like to think so. If only they knew what she was doing to them, then they might question some of the habits they practice on each other. But let's not ruin a perfectly good game by telling them that they are laboratory mice in a running-wheel power generator. With their directed energies combined, they provide a mighty feast.

For decades she has researched the fundamental elements of life. Fearless, she traveled foreign lands and dabbled in all forms of witchery in search of the perfect combination of articles to keep her mind sharp and her body from decaying. From the ancient seas she collected an assortment of crystals which she meticulously channels concentrated beams of radio waves and zooming microwaves that when aimed at the surface of her skin, restore the slacking collagen and elastin that begin to fade with age. She has a greedy hand in the black market trade of exotic herbs and fungi - she even keeps stores of rare coral extracts from the floor of the tropical sea which she bathes in at the break of dawn to rid her body of inflammation.

But these are all just for surface layer upkeep. She discovered long ago where her real strength comes from. And with the investment of time and the clever application of tact, she has made the entire countryside into her playground.

With her power, she spurns confusion and breeds selfishness. She makes many trips different disguises so that no one will mark her presence; for her influence must be felt but not known. Once she has lit the right places - and she always knows where to strike - the whole city is aflame from her putrid force. It does not take long for her to work her magic amongst the blindfolded - they just need a little training - and blind people will follow what feels like a trusted hand.

Once the city is in an uproar and the villagers' heads are flaming, she returns to her home in the forest and enters her charging chamber - the great geometric pyramid that towers above the moss covered oak trees. The pyramids act as a particle resonator of randomly polarized microwave signals which can be converted into electrical energy.

She lies on her immaculate bed in the center of her temple day and night and hungrily absorbs the streaming beams of energy particles that shoot down from the pointed ceiling and bounce into her body as concentrated red light. The structure of the chamber pulls all forms of particles from the atmosphere and channels them into the inside of the structure, where the object in the center is vamped like being struck by red lightning.

For weeks at a time she lays still as a statue so as not to disrupt the flow around her. Her skin tingles as the cells reverse the damages of aging until she feels energized enough to rise. Then she examines the drawing board to strategize her next visit to the village. Should she buzz in the ears of the policymakers, visit the debt-burdened, desperate-for-solutions fathers, or should she teach something wicked to the naive children? The negative energy coming from the villages is still strong, so she doesn't need to do much to keep it going, but the routine is beginning to wear on her.

The feast, as plentiful as it is, does not satisfy her as well as it used to. And no matter how much energy she takes in or how long she confines herself to her bed; lately, she has not been able to convert her stolen energy into anything useful.

She paces the four corners of the chamber and anxiously bites her nails. *Stop that*, she tells herself and examines her hands. Already, they are beginning to wrinkle and blotch with wine stains. Her nails are yellowing. She wrings them out angrily and runs them through her short white hair - the strings of dead cells that give away her true age are past the point of salvaging.

What will she do when the villagers' energy no longer replenishes her? Will she have to drink the blood of virgins like the ancient Greeks? Or maybe coat her temple with crystals to strengthen its channeling power? These could be her next moves. But they are expensive and time consuming.

This is beginning to be a problem.

Contemplating, she explores the fields of energy in the room. With closed eyes she runs her slow hands down the walls and inhales deep, heavy breaths as she feels the cold crevices with searching fingers. *Nothing here!*

Bending to her knees, she crawls onto the sparkling floor and slides her face along the cold quartz stone, sniffing lightly now and again when she feels a change in the air pressure.

"Nothing, nothing, nothing, NOTHING!" She mumbles to the lifeless stone, "give me something good; something *worthy* of my efforts!"

The pyramid answers with an empty echo, reverberating her frigid whispers back at her. Her lips contort at this injustice of wasted time. Rising from the ground, her light feet carry her to the door facing the west, and she creaks it open slightly to feel the changing tide of the October wind.

The sun is just beginning to near the western horizon and its fading light gives everything a soft, blue hue. Colorful leaves tossing in the gust are carried up into the sky, where they are silhouetted in sapphire and then blown over the tops of the trees out of sight. The wind carries the smell of the seasoned forest along with a strange sweet hint of honey nectar, which is out of place in this region. But before she is able to ponder this rarity in the air, a great rumble shakes the tower.

She rushes inside and has to shield her eyes to see what is happening. Meters above, the point of the pyramid is electrified with white beams of bubbling light. They ricochet off of the walls like brilliant buzzing lasers and pop as they collide in the air. As they bounce around, the chamber is filled with a deafening hum that reverberates every molecule of her body.

"WHAT!" she gasps falling to the ground, "Oh my -

what - is this - this is - what? - WHAT! - I - WHAT?" The liver spots vanish and her nails strengthen inside of clenched fists. "WHAT IS THIS POWER?"

But as soon as she utters these things, the lights retreat as sudden as they appeared and the chamber crackles to silence. She lies panting in a pool of sweat on the floor with her arms stretched out staring ahead. It takes a moment for her to realize what just happened.

Jumping to her feet, she excitedly examines the room. Never in her long life has she felt something as strong as this force. It completely knocked her off balance and filled her unlike any source she has ever known. This power came from somewhere nearby - perhaps the village? The woods? - And this enchantress would rather snort anthrax than let this perfect opportunity slip by. She has been searching for something like this, living with eyes wide open, and it seems to have found her on its own!

How wonderful! How wicked! Is this the fabled power she heard of years ago at the last Southern Summit? The power that is strong enough to make you fly? That makes you impenetrable, invincible, and unstoppable! Could it be the very same energy her Southern Sister brushed up against, becoming obsessed when no other witch believed it to be true?

The claim was unfathomable. The Southern Sister professed that her hexagon home burned white like a lightning bolt in a spring storm, and that her blinding radiance that day at the summit was an unexplainable product of some sort of human interaction in her precinct.

"I do not know what they did to create this magnitude of energy," she addressed the silent circle of witches, "but I have never felt anything like it before. Just look at me! I am beautiful!"

This account startled the twelve other witches. It was a painful blow to their pride that the Southern Sister was indeed more youthful than they were. Her self-assured, calm manner was as alien to her usual flimsy posture as her strange new beauty was. But even more unsettling was the idea that the humans had capabilities unknown to them. Their reign is a century in the making and their doctrine toward human beings is nearly as old. This claim challenged the knowledge of the elder witches who created the code by which they exert power to extend their lives.

They sat still in their tall wood-carved chairs, each of them pondering the truth in the matter. Finally, the witch of the Eastern Desert spoke;

"Have you experienced it since that one occasion?"

The Southern Sister shook her head, "No, no. You see, whatever it was that occurred, happened so fast that when I recovered enough to investigate, it had disappeared." She insisted to the twelve unyielding faces, "but I went into the village dressed as a beggar and asked the routine questions to my informers. I admit they were happier than normal, but they did not report anything odd. There were a few travelers in town, but there weren't new ideas, nor were there new hopes. It was very much the same as always."

The witches exchanged incredulous glances.

"Why did you not use white powder gold?" The Gulf Sister asked, a chorus of murmurs agreed, "If it came from humans, like you insist, then the powder would have led you to the most powerful of their kind. It is elementary magic."

The room nodded in agreement.

The Southern Sister snorted and cocked her head, "not all of us can afford such extravagant alchemy. Remember sister, I am the furthest south of the wasted white gold beds. My specialties are local just like the rest of you. But what does this matter? I am telling you, the humans have powers that we do not yet know. I felt it!" Her voice echoed in the chamber.

Then the white-haired witch of the Oakwood Pyramid leaned forward into the light and the company grew silent again. All eyes were on her. She tapped her chin with her index finger and with a sweet smile, she asked "you say it gave you the power to fly?" The Southern Sister respectfully nodded three times and remained silent. "Well, let's see it then. Go on," her voice rose and with the flick of the wrist she demanded, "Fly for us."

"I - I can't anymore."

Some of the witches chuckled, others remained serious.

"Why can't you?" the Pyramid Witch chided, "I thought it was so powerful that it makes you unstoppable."

"It does! But only for a moment. Like I said, it happened so fast…" The Pyramid Witch pursed her lips and the chuckling grew louder. The Southern Sister kept trying over their noise "It is rare!" she shouted, "There is nothing like it in our history books! I am not making this up! I-"

The Pyramid Witch raised her hand and the Southern Sister stopped talking. An authoritative hush fell over the group. "Is it not true, Southern Sister, that you have also discovered a mammoth cave of calcite crystal?" The Gulf Witch gasped and every one moved to the edge of their chairs. "And you have been hording its healing power for at least a decade, growing stronger and younger while the rest of us rely on pathetic human waste!" The Southern Sisters face turned pale and the Witch rose to her feet, "HOW DARE YOU HIDE YOUR NATURAL SUPPLIES IN A TIME OF FAMINE! YOUR PATHETIC COVER STORY - HUMANS?! - WAS A WASTE OF TIME. MAYBE YOU CAN AFFORD TO WASTE IT WHILE YOU SLEEP IN A BED OF CRYSTALS EVERY NIGHT, BUT THE REST OF US CAN NOT TAKE CHANCES. YOU ARE A SNEAK THEIF AND A LIAR. YOUR COVER IS BLOWN!"

The summit closed with the Southern Sister's calcite cave divided thirteen ways, and the account of white human power became a joke among the lighthearted, and a myth among the superstitious. But be it jest or fable, at this time, decades later, the Pyramid Witch remembers the occasion well. It didn't matter if the Southern Sister spoke the truth about human potential; it was of the utmost importance to uphold the Code of the Witches, which was to harness only the stable red energy… at least that is how she wanted to appear that day.

Salivating with replenished energy and a wetted appetite, she vaults onto her oak bed. Holding her breath, she snatches the precious purple velvet satchel from a hanging wire line above the bed frame. Lingering for a moment to stare at the embroidered eye of Horus, she snaps her fingers above the wick of a candle and it illuminates her ecstatic eyes. With no hesitation, she takes a pinch of the satchels rare contents into her open right hand, forcefully clenches her fist seven times, smacks the palm of her hand over the clenched fist and then stares at the material. The fine white powder is light as air in her palm. It faintly glitters in the candle light, and with an ever expanding smile, she blows it over the steady flame.

The dust sizzles through the fire, hovers in the air and expands as a thick cloud, and then begins to shape shift before her eyes.

"White Powder Gold, White Powder Gold. Tell what must be told, tell what must be told," she chants.

The churning element cloud is a uniquely powerful platinum group superconductor. She patiently waits as its monatomic molecules traverse other dimensions through fluctuating magnetic wormholes that allow for hyper-communication.

It starts to spiral in quick circular motions, making ringlets above her white head. The atomically altered

Egyptian gold is a form of electromagnetically null dark matter that interlaces with DNA, so as it circles in the air after being heated, its molecules search for the strongest bonds of DNA it can find.

As if struck by the wind, the cloud zooms across the chamber and paints a white circle on the south corner of the western wall.

"Oh…" she ponders as she crosses the room to see the formation. The dust particles shimmer in the candlelight. "A circle. A perfect circle." She muses, "But what is it?" She examines it closer, her nose almost touching the crystallized powder. "What does it mean?"

From the leaning bookshelf she removes a worn book, one from a series of dusty leather bounds, titled *Humans and Synchronicity.* Turning to the index she finds what she is looking for: *The Formations of WPG and what they Mean pg. 399.* "Haha! Perfect."

Flipping to the beginning of the chapter, her eyes flit across images of squares, stars, pentagons, eagles, hares, mushrooms, and shields. Finally, at the end of the chapter, a stark white circle identical to the one on her western wall stares back up at her. She pauses for a moment and reads the passage:

Although there is no solid evidence to support the existence of a circular white powder gold (WPG) formation, throughout history, several Witches claim to have witnessed crystallization in a radial, symmetrical form. The accounts given by those who were sane after their encounter can be summarized as follows:

The circle indicates a continuous, eternal function of untapped human capability. One that exists, but has been forgotten by those in authority because the only way to harness the energy of the circle is to break the circle; a difficult and very dangerous task. The circle represents two halves that are bonded together on two ends (like two crescent moon magnets). Each half contains a human being that, by some enchantment or spell, has bonded with an opposite. This mysterious union, if actually true, is believed to be the most valuable energy source in existence.

*A WARNING to any who come across a WPG circle formation. BEWARE!
All interviewed witnesses who have attempted to break the circle are now considered mad. Hence the credibility issues of the accounts.

With a confident smile, the Pyramid Witch closes the book. Holding it at arm's length, she smiles again, "Mad!" She says to herself, "I would be mad not to go after this opportunity." Walking to the full length mirror she takes a long, hard look at herself.

Am I ready for this? Her reflection has never looked better. *I must be. I am only growing older.* She glances at her fresh fingernails. *But I must refine my methods. For this to work, the choice of which half of the circle receives the treatment will have to be made at random. Which half will be tested first?*

After a moment to ponder, she withdraws a large gold coin from her bureau and, placing it on the table with a pocket knife in hand, she scrapes the letters X and Y on opposite sides. Then she stands back and with her thumb, flicks the coin high into the air. The coin clatters to the floor and she leans down to examine it. Y, it reads.

"Subject Y it is!" and turning back to the mirror, "Let me show you how to break a spell."

West of the pyramid, the hazy blue sunset lights a blossoming clearing in the western realm of the wood. Like brilliant fireflies late at night, the sprinklings of white irises dazzle the deep sapphire sea of grass. The crickets' ring saturates the valley. Over their chorus, a shaggy-haired bloke plays the harmonica to his maiden. He holds her gaze as she dances in a merry circle around the flowers. Her honey nectar scent fills the clearing with exotic dreams it never dreamt of before they came along.

In a lacey, cream-colored dress with a silk ribbon tied in her long autumn-orange hair, the maiden nibbles on a piece of sour grass as she sings her favorite prayer of Saint Frances to his tune.

"Make me an instrument of peace;
Where there is hatred, let me sow love;
Where there is injury, pardon;
Where there is doubt, faith;
Where there is despair, hope;
Where there is darkness, light;
And where there is sadness, joy.
Grant that I may not so much seek to be consoled as to console;
To be understood, as to understand;
To be loved, as to love;
For it is in giving that we receive,
It is in pardoning that we are pardoned,
And it is in dying that we are born to Eternal Life."

She finishes with a bow and a curtsey which he smiles at, and then she continues packing away the remains of their lunch into the travel bags leaning against an oak tree. The rations and camp gear have taken them a long way since they began their journey two weeks ago, but soon they will have to make a stop to replenish their supplies before they are left with nothing but a sack of rice.

It has been dangerous in the wood so far, with more than one tight situation to escape from - starvation and wild animals - but every obstacle brings them closer together, solidifying their bond, making them stronger. Humming to his tune, she closes the pack and dances back over to him. She slides to the petal covered ground and rests her happy head in his lap.

"Do you ever wonder why things are this way?" she says through her teeth as she nibbles the stem of a flower.

He lowers his harmonica and looks down at her upturned face. That face! The face of a natural goddess with kaleidoscope eyes that read into the very mechanics of your mind and cherry lips that speak only wisdom; wisdom far too complex for a girl of her age. Who is he to deserve such perfection? Who is he to carry the love of one so pure? So innocent. So young. His little Aphrodite.

She continues, "Do you ever wonder why strange, unexpected things happen? And why we let them happen?" She meticulously shreds a flower petal with her fingers and looks around the woods.

"I mean, take this situation for example. So many strange events had to take place for us to be here; events that were seemingly meaningless at the time, yet, critical in each of our lives, built on each other moment after moment, time after time, again and again until this present situation came to be. How did this happen? How did it come from what was… from being nothing into being something?"

The look on his face says that he is thinking about what she is saying. She loves it when he listens to her ramblings. Such a brilliant mind he has. Why aren't more people as open and caring as he is? Why is it too easy to misunderstand people's intent? It should be a joy for everyone to get to know someone of opposite mentality.

"I suppose that some of these unexpected things can happen only when the moment is just right, and those involved are ready and willing to accept it." She muses, kicking her bare feet high in the air, "It is almost like, for me to be able to accept it, I have to first give up my pride, my ego, and my self-centeredness. And THEN, after I have let go of all of that nonsense, I am finally free to live in the moment and love wholeheartedly."

She sits up and takes his hand into hers, "I don't know... what do you think?"

"That makes sense on an emotional level," he traces the life-line on her palm, "Though; I think that whenever a life changing event takes place, it is opportunity meeting preparation. You should recognize it when you see it. Like I recognized you for what you are when we met - you are an apparition - or like how I knew that I wanted to be a musician the first time I picked up a guitar. It just made sense; as if I knew ahead of time that these things were right for me. And I was ready for them.

You always have a sense of control in whatever you do. Acceptance is only a part of the process. You made it happen regardless of whether you accept it or not."

Temperature rising, he moves closer. With gentle hands he cups her back and slowly lowers her body into the green grass. As she folds down, she pulls the fabric of his shirt so that he comes with her. He rests his head on her chest and listens as her lungs take in air.

"You should always be in control," he whispers, "you always are in control." His lips brush her skin, "I am the creator of everything around me. And you are the creator of everything around you."

An owl hoots at the dark edge of the forest and its oval eyes are all that can be seen in the fading light. The creatures of the night begin to awaken from their slumber and their noises rise around them.

"But what about God?" She asks as she catches her breath, "How does his spirit play into this?"

"I don't think you need to wonder anymore, love," he reassures through a deep kiss. "Everything is exactly as it should be. And it will always be this way if you just let go."

Giggling, she moves away and tries to discern his face in the dimming light. "You are too good with words.

You are trying to shut me up with your lyrics! I know it!"

"Babe, if you are wondering what the secrets are to the universe then you are wandering down a cursed path." he reaches out for her, "The answer is; there is no answer."

"Uhuh," she laughs, "I see right through you! You just don't have an opinion."

He laughs at her and pulls her closer, breathing his love into her neck and she brushes it off. He sits up taller, "Okay, It's more like this," he muses, "I am God." The maiden scrunches her face at him so he continues, "you are God too. We are creators. Look! That journal you always carry with you, someone created that. And the music I play I create. Most people see God as distant and untouchable. I see myself as God and try to touch others."

"Wow. So I am touching God right now?" she teases.

"Well, in a way, yes."

"All hail the omnipresent, omnipotent God of perfection! Here before my very eyes. Is this a vision? Am I like Saul? Should I change my name?"

"Pshh. Listen," he sighs, finding the right words. "God is perfection, right? Well how can God be perfect if Satan exists? Didn't God create everything, so didn't God create Satan? Did perfection spawn imperfection? If so, then I think we are supposed to test both the light and the darkness. The overarching "God," as we call it, is both light and dark and it is all just a metaphor for what goes on inside us humans. We all have darkness and we all have light. We are all creators. We are all Gods."

"So, you are saying that we are Gods yet there is also a bigger God? Something that put everything into motion."

"Exactly. I desire to meet the being who put the forces to motion. Is that being me? Who is Satan? Is Satan negative or positive or neither? Satan represents whatever I want it to represent. It is an entity that can be filled. Say it with me. *I love Satan.*"

"No!"

"No? Okay, then say *I love say ten.*"

"No way!" She shakes her head, "If there is a light and a dark inside us, then I want to be the light. What good can embracing darkness bring?"

"Again, there is no good and evil. God is both. You are both. Unity is the ultimate goal. Unite the positive and the negative forces and you become God. You are God. You are both negative and positive. Just be both."

"I would rather just be me."

"You don't know who you are yet." His voice lowers and he leans in close to her again, "You don't know what you are capable of. I can help with this but you haven't been ready. I think you are almost there." His hand moves to caress her thigh. "Giving in is one of the sweetest sensations. Give in." His intense gaze makes her dizzy. "Here is to me giving in to you," he kisses her forehead, "giving in to me," he kisses her cheek, "giving in to this insanity."

They lay down into the grass and she is overwhelmed by the passion behind his kisses. She almost forgets herself. It takes the hoot of the owl for her to shake back to reality.

"Really now," she jumps up and brushes off the petals laughing lightly, dancing away from him, "It is almost full night." She straightens her hair and offers a hand to the bloke. "We should head toward the group of lights we passed a few miles ago. It looked like a village. It would be a nice change to sleep inside." She laughs at this groan, "Not that I don't love the outdoors."

Knocking the dirt off his knees he grumbles, and throws the tote over his shoulder. "Okay fine. Let's go. Just as long as there is a bed large enough for the both of us!"

He swings her into his arms and she kicks and

giggles as they disappear from the clearing leaving nothing but trampled grass as a mark of their presence. Behind the trees, just beyond the clearing, the owl follows silently.

The sun has set by the time they hike to the outskirts of the town. As the lights grow brighter, the trees begin to thin out, and between the barky trunks they see the first dwellings. Low to the ground, the houses are held together by nails, plywood and rope, and look like they have been lived in for many generations. The roofs are slanted and sunken with missing shingles, the brick is crumbling, and as the couple comes closer, they notice that the houses appear to be missing doors. No, the doors of every house on the lane are open. As the pair pass by the first of these, they can't help but look across the unkempt yard, through the open door frame.

Nestled around a cracked fireplace, a huddle of middle-aged individuals chatter in low voices, each holding a festive party cup. Above their heads a few bright orange streamers sway in the slight breeze that drafts through the house, tickling the fire. They seem to be discussing something rather serious despite the colorful ornaments. Then the hunched partiers sense a change in the air and turn to look outside, toward the moving shadows in the lane. Their conversation tapers out, and they blink in surprise at what they see.

In a slit of firelight against the black of the forest, the two stand out like a lightning bolt in a clear night sky; a pair of young travelers that seem to glow despite the darkness. Where did they come from? What are they? But before the residents can figure out it out, the couple hurries up the pathway leaving the shabby partiers in confusion.

Shrugging off the villagers' open stares, the couple assumes they must have startled them by surprise and smirk to each other as they travel deeper into the neighborhood. There must be some kind of festival going on, because as the shanties are traded for brick and motor structures, all is decorated with ribbons and flags, and every home is brimming with revelers. A few of them notice the vagabonds, and upon seeing them, they pause their antics to stare as they pass by.

It is strange to the couple that as much as the town is dressed for celebration, there is an underlying current of misery and despair in the citizens. Each home has its doors open, but the people look stiff and a feeling of paranoia seeps from the door frames as if they think the people in the very room are plotting against them; family and friends are not to be trusted.

The bloke and the maiden draw close to each other as they approach a block party that extends into the town center. Orange and gold banners flap on flag poles that line the cobblestone avenue. From the canvas canopies of the bazaar up ahead, dried mushrooms and carved gourds sway in the breeze. Weary panderers beckon every passerby to have a look at their dried goods for sale or for trade. Bottles of wine are uncorked and mugs clank together as they toast to each other's good health. But beneath uneasy smiles, they imagine how many headstones will be added to the cemetery by spring.

The bloke grabs her hand instinctively and they edge into the crowd in silence. They are ushered onward into the city shoulder-to-shoulder with the tipsy revelers. Now and then someone will glare in their direction, or pull away as if the couple is unpleasant or painful to the eyes.

"Here," he says uneasily leading her gaze to his face, "Let's go to the market over there. Get what we need and get out of here."

She agrees, "And it would be a good idea to find a place to stay." He raises his eye brows. "I don't mind sleeping here as long as it isn't a common room. I'm sure we will meet some friendlies." She smiles a hopeful half-smile. Moving away from the crumbling homes and townhouses, they head toward the shadow of the blackened bell tower; leaving a street of onlookers in their wake.

The bazaar is teeming with last minute fall bargainers; those who did not carefully save their summer stores in preparation and spent their time gambling and drinking away their problems before the change of season. These are the ones who have the most to fear; for if they are not able to gather what they need before the first fall of snow, then they have to fear their neighbors' rightful suspicions of thievery and trickery. They dread the swiftness of change that results in fast, unstoppable ruin.

They haggle, they argue, they blame others for their self-perpetuating misfortune. No one is free from judgment. Everyone must face this terrible circumstance of desperate want - even those who are more prepared for change. They push each other out of their way, knocking merchandise over. They bite at each other's faces with impatience, pretending to wait while they would rather kick the person in front of them. They buy things they don't even want just because it looks like there will be a scarcity soon.

These people weren't born this way, they were bred this way. Even when scarcity proves to be an illusion of the market, they buy into it. Sometimes, the peddlers will purposefully leave most of their stock at home and then convince their costumers that they are almost out. They inflate their pockets without any real lack of goods. And sometimes, the costumers will pretend they have less money than they really do, and they beg for what they already can afford. Everyone works in agreement with the system and chuckle to themselves as they believe they have swindled the swindlers in every deal.

Do they grow tired of it? Hardly. Haggling is what makes them feel alive. It is all they know. It gives them purpose. They do it out of habit and encouragement from the town leaders. Even if they were tired of it, there is nothing they could do because their system of exchange was created generations before they were born and their leaders follow the rule of law. And since most of their tax money goes into fixing the debt their system has created, there is little money left to teach the youngest in the town. So there are no new ideas; only a continuous cycle of doubt and depression fueled by ignorance. But they will find someone to blame. Someone will be punished for the misfortune of the masses.

The vendors look up from their stands. The hunt for a scapegoat is in their eyes. Could these strangers suffice? These strangers are strange indeed. As the two meander cautiously beneath the moth-eaten tents, they keep an eye out for fresh vegetables, spices, and small necessities and hardly notice the glares they receive. The shelves behind the weary salesmen are nearly bare but the two exchange hopeful looks. There must be something worth their time around here.

Between the stall of the butcher and the tailor, for a brief second the maiden catches a glimpse of something bright orange. It is dark, so she squints to be sure. Carrots! Exactly what she wants. She turns to the bloke, who has his eye on the meat market, and placing a hand on his shoulder she says, "You hold a space and get us some jerky if you can, I will be right back."

"Wha- yea ok."

Leaving him to join a long line of customers, she walks through a narrow space in the dark between the stalls and approaches a canvas tent reinforced with open faced oak beams. The cold cobblestone around the stall is lit with a soft sprinkling of little orbs that are cast from over a dozen large blue lanterns with circles cut in the tin encasement. The walls are decorated with exotic patterned draperies and there is a light scent of burning sage held within the tent. On the countertop, a wide selection of bright vegetables - the freshest she has seen so far - cover every space, and behind a grate of gourds, a young woman with striking white hair wipes dirt from a giant pumpkin with a wet rag. She notices the maiden, thumbs her hair behind her ears and slinks around the grates behind the counter. This vendor has a strange, unnatural glow to her milky skin, making her features slightly fuzzy; and she is stunningly beautiful despite her humble garb of a shabby grey jumper.

The vendor leans over the wood panel and purrs, "Good Samhain," locking eyes with the maiden, "what can I do for a lovely traveler?" Shifting slightly, the maiden tries to look back at the countertop, but she can't seem to pull her mind back to herself. Be it focus or intent, this woman's resonating energy demands recognition.

"I uh," she clears her throat; "I would like a bushel of those c-carrots." She stammers and lands her pack on the counter with a thud. Drawing a breath to reclaim her presence; "enough to fill this bag for two people for a week."

The vendor's burgundy lips turn up to a slight grin, "hmmm!" and she licks them in pause. Turning silently to the wooden grate behind her she unlatches the top and pulls out a handful of large, bright orange carrots. She gazes at them for a moment as if they are connected to something, and then it clicks. Holding them up to the maidens face, she exclaims, "Well look at this! They are exactly the color of your hair! Remarkable! You must have known. Our choices!" Pressed against her cool skin, the produce is the very burnt orange of the maiden's hair.

Drawing back to investigate, "well, look at that!" the maiden amuses. She looks from the sight at hand, and locking eyes with the vendor again, she is unable to collect herself a proper response. The vendor notices this and draws out her words in a smooth voice, "what a beautiful color. The most striking I think I have ever seen worn on a person." She hands the carrots to the maiden, who smiles warmly in thanks. "These carrots will give that porcelain skin a nice glow, like an internal summer tan."

She pauses, scanning over the maiden's upright posture and travel-worn, yet collected look. Her eyes land on her pink lips. "And here," she says pulling out a satchel of sliced roots with a twinkle in her eye, "chew these after a meal and you will have fresh breath while on your journey. I'm sure you and your travel companion will appreciate this!"

The maiden tucks the carrots and the satchel away into the pack, restraining a laugh, "I haven't heard any complaints, but I guess it could be helpful." She tries to look away to break the connection but the vendor isn't done yet.

"I also have a balm that will brighten up your eyes." The vendor uncorks a milky solution and dabs it on a clean cloth from beneath the counter. Leaning in she cups the maidens face and gently smoothes it onto her skin beneath her eyes. "And if you tuck your hair up like this," she curls a lock up and over the maidens ear and swiftly pins it in with a ornate silver flower clip, "you can appear more open and inviting. Look!" She hands her a mirror.

"Oh wow!" the maiden exclaims. "This is a beautiful clip."

"The clip is a foreign import and has a very rare design, yes, but look how lovely *you* are."

"Thank you," the maiden blushes and tries to lower the mirror, but the vendor holds it in place.

"Love," she insists, "Look at *yourself.* I am an expert in all things beautiful and have helped many in enhancing what they have been given. But *you* have a natural beauty that should be admired."

The maiden hesitates, and then obeys, peering back into the depths of the mirror. At first she sees just herself as she always is, just her. But then she begins to notice how the color of her eyes seem to ripple pleasantly between yellow with flecks of gold and the tiniest hint of green, and how her shining hair appears to be in motion by the reflection of the natural shine and the play of the orb lights. Then she notices the red wine stains on the vendor's outstretched hands and her cracked fingernails.

The vendor covers them embarrassed, "That is from an unfortunate occurrence at a campfire. No problem for me really. Oh but I have so much more, so many more balms at home. These you can have for free." Handing her the clip and bottle.

"I can't-"

"Please," her eyes glowing, "for someone of your magnitude, it couldn't have a more worthy owner."

"They are wonderful. Thank you," tucking them away in her bag.

"Now to the groceries." She turns around and shuffles through the cases, adding vegetables and dried goods to a sack. Behind her, on top of a shelf of multicolored vials perches a wide-eyed barn owl who watches the maiden intently. "This should do," the vendor says handing her the heavy bag, "that will be five coins please."

The maiden frowns at the price but takes out her coin purse and pays the vendor her due. "Believe me sweetie," the vendor adds with a sparkle in her eye, "this is the best deal you will get for the quality of the crop. And, before you go, let me make a suggestion." Her voice lowers and she leans in, beckoning the maiden closer. The maiden obliges and studies her strange face.

"More than likely, the local inns will be booked tonight for Samhain. And if you visit them and find there are no vacancies, then come back here to my booth before I pack up and I will let you stay in my guest house. It is just a suggestion." Her voice drops even lower, "this is not a good night to camp in the old forest. It gets very unpredictable toward the end of the night, very dangerous, especially for anyone from out of town."

"Right, thank you," the maiden pulls away and tosses the sack over her shoulder. "I will keep that in mind." Turning to leave she wonders what she meant by unpredictable.

Under the yellow lamps at the meat market, the maiden finds the bloke stalking away from the counter with a large bundle under his left arm, avoiding being seen by the black-toothed butcher. He cups her elbow and leads her around a corner and away a few yards.

"What did you find?" He asks, happy to see her.

"Carrots and a few other things," she stretches up to kiss him. "You blasted through that line! I expected to find you right where I left you. Hey, where are we going?"

"Just over here." A dark corner.

"How much was the jerky? The prices are horribly inflated here."

"Wasn't too bad," he answers vaguely.

"Too bad as in… how much?"

"I got the best possible discount."

"And what was that?"

"Just the right amount that we can afford."

"Which is?"

"You are always asking questions."

"You are always avoiding answers! Let's see what you got then," she giggles, "maybe I can guess the price."

She reaches for the bundle under his arm and he hesitates, but obliges. Wrapped in one of his sweaters is a overabundance of dried beef jerky and a fresh slab of thin cut bacon. The bloke helps her hold the bundle open and waits for her reaction.

"This is," she starts slowly, "way more than we can afford. How did you get this?"

"We deserve this," he watches the implication dawn on her.

"You stole it?"

He wraps the bundle up and ties the arm sleeves around it together. Opening the pack on her back, he drops the bundle in, but not without noticing the satchel and bottle she got from the vendor.

"The world operates on the availability of resources," he explains while fastening the pack, "If you have them, you survive. If you don't, you die. I want you to have whatever you need." He senses her disapproval so he wraps his arms around her waist and she leans in, "I'll do anything for your love no matter the cost. And you know I don't eat bacon. That is for you!"

She stands firm for a moment and then; "It is good to know we won't be hungry for a while." He turns her around and they embrace. Something catches his eye as he pulls back.

Up the street, rounding the corner, a throng of tired villagers with torches held high above their heads march side-by-side. After them, a group of horn blowers march in sync, blowing a slow mournful tune. Beyond that, a huddle of small pale children sprinkle dead flowers on the ground beneath them. The parade passes by the ogling couple, and they notice through the dark the partakers have skeletons painted on their skin in white paint - even the children.

"Is this part of the celebration or has someone died?" The bloke whispers to the maiden. With the low hung heads of the villagers it is hard to tell. One woman's feet drag on the cobblestones as if she isn't conscious of walking at all, a man rings a bell in beat but grinds his teeth angrily looking as if he would rather be anywhere but there, a little girl elbows a boy to her left and he calls her a curt name.

The maiden shakes her head darkly, "looks like they aren't in the mood. Weird. I would just drop out."

"Or not agree to do it at all. Doesn't look fun. Let's search for an inn. I can't watch this anymore."

"Agreed," says the maiden as he takes her hand and

leads them down an alleyway, out of view.

But the mood of the parade doesn't disappear around the corner. The butcher shoots them a venomous look as he hacks deep rifts into beef shank with dull cleaver, elbow deep in blood. Caught in the wrong moment, a spray of blood flecks the maidens cheek and she quickly wipes it off, shivering in disgust.

They duck down a small street that leads to the town hall. As a raggedy woman brushes by carrying a decorative torch, she kicks a screeching cat toward them and spits on the ground at their shock.

"What is with these people?" Whispers the bloke, and jumps out of the way of an old woman heaving her dirty dish water out of her window in their direction. "I feel like they are aiming for us!"

Stepping over the slimy puddle she plugs her nose, "Yea, you know, I almost forgot to tell you. Someone warned me to stay out of the village tonight."

"Was it the same friendly who gave you that?" He touches the clip in her hair. She gives her hair a toss to show it off. "It's nice," he continues, "what did he tell you?"

"*She* told me that things get unpredictably dangerous on the nights of this festival."

"Samhain-"

"-Yea, how did you-"

"-I can ask questions too."

She smiles, "Of course you can. Well anyway it is supposed to be worse off for people from out of town. She was really vague about it, but she suggested we -" Suddenly something very large and fast comes rumbling straight at her. "WOAH!!" She screams and throws herself against a brick wall and is narrowly missed by a rocketing wheelbarrow full of trout.

"Out of th-way!" bellows a stout, bald man shoving the wheelbarrow at a careless speed.

"Watch it!" The bloke yells after him but isn't acknowledged. "There is something wrong with these people!" He half runs after him but slows down when he compares their size and sees he would probably lose, "Come on!" He urges the maiden forward.

Walking faster, the narrow street opens up to a wide courtyard. A hazy layer of smog holds the still air and a shifting crowd sways and mingles in every corner. To the right they spot a sign hanging with a quarter moon engraved in the rotting wood that reads Lunestar Inn. Single windows stretch five stories high above it, lit with flickering oil lamps. The front door is closed and appears to be locked.

After knocking, there is movement behind the red curtains to the left of the door. Someone pulls the curtain aside and quickly peers through at them. A gruff voice sounds through the glass, "What do ya want?"

"This is an inn right?" the bloke asks incredulously.

The voice coughs and hacks, then replies, "We're full."

"Are there any other inns close by?" the maiden says hopefully.

The voice pauses, "You can try The Coventry on Hill Top. Though I wouldn't stay there if I were respectable." The curtain opens more and a pair of large, sunken eyes study them. "No. They are probably full anyhow."

A loud screech coming from somewhere in the square makes them whirl around. At the foot of the clock tower, a mass of revelers are closing in on what looks like a pair of fighting women. One of them has a firm grip on the other's wrist. "Take her hand!" She yells over crowd, "Take her right hand, the thief!" The captive woman moans something but it is drowned by the cheers from the enclosing mob. She is hoisted up into the air over their jeering faces, and disappears behind torches and banners.

The man behind the curtain clears his throat abruptly, "NO. I can't help you. Go away," and he blows out his lantern.

Exchanging fearful looks they back into the doorway of the Lunestar Inn as the mob saunters by. A few of the revelers point curious fingers at the couple and whisper to each other.

"I think we should move." the maiden says, gripping the blokes arm.

"Where do we go?"

"To the vendor. She said we could stay with her. Come on."

In one move off of the step they are swallowed by the mob. Their volition is of no consequence in the turbulent masses. With arms cleaving to each other, they are thrust forward, almost tripping to keep in step. In front of them, a man goes down and they are heaved over the trampled body. The bloke lifts the maiden off the ground just in time to avoid her stepping on his head. Then they are smashed into each other as the rumbling mob bottlenecks through an alley. On the other side, a hand covered in scratches reaches backward from atop the crowd and grabs a wad of the maiden's hair. She is pulled to meet the ghastly upside-down face of condemned thief.

"Help me! HELP ME!" the woman shrieks in short breaths. "Help me! They will KILL ME!"

The maiden wraps her fingers around the woman's wrist and with her other hand yanks her hair out of her grasp. As the orange strands are pulled from her fingers, the woman lands hold of the hair clip and yanks it up to look at it. Staring at the clip the woman turns a shade paler. "I'm a dead woman," she mumbles and is carried away.

"Quick!" the bloke shouts as a gap opens between the frenzy, "GO!" Together they dart full speed around charging feet and fist-pumping arms. Wave upon wave of townspeople flood the street as if called by some greater force. They march into the market place and the couple dives into an abandoned tent full of musky, stacked furs. They quickly close the flap and fasten it tight. The stampede muffled, both register the shock on each other's faces but don't know what to do. The torch bearing mob presses in on the tent as they pass by, illuminating the canvas from the outside.

In the orange glow, the maiden's eyes begin to water, "we should stay here as long as we can." The bloke paces a moment and then pulls back a corner of the flap to see what is going on outside.

The eyes of the revelers are dilated. They carry with them an unfathomable hate. Terror seizes him at the sight of these new specimens - the mob floats several more struggling captives.

Turning back to the maiden his mouth gapes and he struggles to find the words. "We cannot stay here."

The roar outside is almost defeating. The air crackles with kinetic confusion. Spirits of despair have awoken and have spurned fanatical vengeance. The mob carries their captives to the edge of the wood where they disappear in shadow and finality. The couple hide in a mound of fir not sure of what to do. The scent of smoke reaches their noses and the bloke starts.

"Come on! Let's get out of here."

"To where!"

"The forest."

"No! They will find us."

"Then where? We can hide."

"Don't you see! They are taking *them* there."

"We can't stay here!"

And as he speaks there is a crash not a yard from their tent. A furious glow lights the room. Small licks of flame sneak under the canvas begin to climb the walls. Dread fills them and they jump to their feet and dash around stacks of fur, cans of salts and emollient. Coughing through smoke, their tent catches fire and they exit onto the street again. And the revelers surround them.

She watches the chaos from a second story balcony across the street. Through the billowing smoke spirals she studies her targets. The couple rises and sinks from view, engulfed in the swarm. Their eyes dart for places to escape. The witch climbs onto the fire escape where they can see her, "HERE!" she bellows over the crowd. "Lady! This way!" her hand extends into space.

The maiden coughs a lungful of smoke and points at the white-haired woman on the fire-escape. The vendor beckons her again with shouts and wild hand gestures. The rumbling mob is still churning - an impassable obstacle between them.

Then she catches the bloke's attention. He sees what she is pointing out and surges through the maze of wreckage, pulling his girlfriend behind him. The mob has so many hands to terrorize. They push against him, catch the collar of his shirt and try to drag him into the current again. The vendor's hand is only a few paces away. He cuts through a gap and then grabs the maiden by the waist, hoisting her into the air. The women lock hands.

The world swirls a little in the vendor's eyes. She has what she needs in her very grasp! Leaning back to occupy all of her weight, she heaves the maiden up. The little redhead swings her knees onto the wobbling platform and quickly stands. Together they reach out for the man below.

He crashes onto the landing. As he scrambles to his feet, the vendor is already bounding up the first stairs toward the second landing. They rush after her without pausing. Rust dusts onto their heads from the winding steps above. Below, the masses still mingle and cry for out for blood.

Clanking on the steps above tells them she is still up ahead, but they can't see the white soles of her shoes anymore. A cool breeze deafens the screaming below. Turning up the last stairwell they see a ladder on the far end of the last landing. They take it step-by-step, avoiding the missing rungs and they land their feet on the tar-coated roof.

Across the platform she stands silhouetted against the orange blaze. Her white hair whips the air and from the shadow her face speaks.

"Come closer. We are safe for only a moment," She glances down at the masses in the streets.

"Can you explain *what* is going on down there?" the bloke interjects, "this town is crazy! What are they doing to those people?"

The vendor takes a breath and pauses to consider what to say. "It is customary to give offerings to the White Goddess before the winter. The festival makes the residents anxious to please her. After last year's losses to starvation, we got carried away this year. I hope they don't destroy everything."

"It looks more like madness than anxiousness!" the maiden exclaims.

"It can be the same thing," the vendor adds.

"But what is this White Goddess?" The bloke steps forward, "do *you* worship her?"

"I do not need to. My crops come from abroad. But come! We do not have much time now."

And with a swish she turns and leaps off the ledge, vanishing into the dark. The couple rushes forward and peers down the crack between the two buildings - nothing is there but a trash bin and a scruffy cat. Then they notice a flash of white glistening from the next roof over.

"This way!" it calls out to them.

"She jumped the roof! She's a nutter!" the bloke exclaims in wonderment.

"Yes. Well," the maiden replies. "I guess we don't have much of a choice but to follow."

"We have a choice-"

"Come on!" With that the maiden sails into the air, landing deftly on the other side. The bloke gapes after her. Then he jumps down too. Before they can settle themselves, the vendor is already on the next roof top. So they follow, descending the city from the top down.

As the buildings become lower and further apart, they climb down a tree on a sunken roof and make their way on foot. Most of the villagers have disappeared into the forest. And that is where they appear to be heading.

They fly down the lane, by more shanties; their tenants vacant. At the end of the lane there is a trail. She leads them up into wooded hills on a winding path. The air is tight in their lungs but they rush on. The trees grow close and knotted roots loop out of the earth making the path a blind hop-scotch game. Far away there are torches visible, hundreds of them passing quickly down a sister path. They can just barely make out the figures. The paths are parallel for a moment and they can see the mob rushing by with their captives surfing on top.

"Where are they going?" the bloke calls ahead to the vendor.

Her eyes flash back at him, "to a burn pit. It is almost time for the bone-fire."

"Bone-fire," he whispers to himself and shivers.

The path becomes thinner and harder to follow, and is coming closer to the mob. Without a lantern they aren't likely to be seen, but still, there is fear in the couple's hearts. The ground slopes up and as they round a bend they look back at where the torches were last seen. A blood-curdling scream echoes through the forest. And then a spot in the distance is filled with bright light. A cheer fills the night.

The maiden reaches the bloke's hand in the dark

and they break into a run again. It is hard to see ahead on the path. The vendor knows the route well and isn't lingering for them. With their free hands in front of them and the bloke in the lead, they just barely dodge tree trunks. As they dart around a very large one, the ground gives out and the bloke tumbles down a sharp hill and into a bush.

"Are you okay!" the maiden shouts making her way around the roots.

He is groaning under a shrub, holding his left ankle. "I think," he pants, "I think I twisted my ankle. On one of those damned roots."

"Oh babe!" She lands next to him and feels the damage. "Can you walk on it?"

"I think. I think." He leans on a tree for support and pushes himself into a standing position. Gingerly, he takes a step. Pain shoots up his left leg and his eyes water, but he stays standing.

"Come on, lean on me. You are going to have to try."

He wraps his left arm over her shoulders and they take a few steps together. Breaking out into a sweat, he manages to hop lightly on his damaged leg, in a kind of three-legged walk with the maiden. They have lost their speed, but at least he can move. Up ahead the path leads into a moonlit patch of shrubbery. The distant cheering fades into crickets. They keep walking as fast as they can. Time passes without them noticing. There is still no sign of the vendor, nothing but the sense that she is still speeding along ahead somewhere.

The path winds down into an open grove of oak trees. Their heavy boughs stretch higher than any trees they have seen so far, and some of them rest on the ground, snaking out in the dirt. The forest floor becomes soft with leaves and they pad over it in their awkward walk.

The air becomes noticeably different, like there is static holding it in motion. They feel somehow lighter, stronger; and the hairs on the maidens head lift ever so slightly without her knowledge.

Up head, a light is discernable between the boughs. A warm glow from a lantern lights the covered porch of a large wooden cottage. There is a stick of incense burning in a flower pot next to a post. The door is open just the like others closer to the town, but as they cautiously pass by, the maiden notices a note tacked to the door frame.

"Wait," she slows their pace. The bloke is too tired to care what they do, he was just focusing on moving. She leans him against the post and he watches, panting as she takes the piece of paper off of the wall and holds it in the light.

"To the couple," she reads aloud, "Go no further tonight. This is my guest house and I have left it open for you. Make yourselves at home. I will see you in the morning." At the bottom of the page, the vendor signed the message with a dash and a triangle. But the vendor is not there.

Just as the maiden is about to ask the bloke what he thinks, he starts to slide down the post in a faint. She rushes over and catches him before he hits the ground. His ankle has swollen the size of a small melon and his face is sickly green. He is quickly fading out. Not knowing what else to do, she swings his left arm back around her shoulder and drags him across the porch through the open door.

Inside there is a wide, wood-fitted, half-circle room with a small kitchen tucked into the left corner; soft furniture lay around a cold fireplace in the center and there are several doors that lead off to different rooms. One of them is open.

"Come on," the maiden encourages him, "just a little bit further."

He tries to rouse himself to walk, but doesn't have the energy. She leads them into the bedroom and heaves him onto the quilt-covered bed. He grunts in pain as she straightens him out and places a pillow under his head. His ankle is throbbing, his head is throbbing, he can't see clearly so he closes his eyes.

She runs to the kitchen and opens every drawer till she finds several rags, and soaking them in water from a carafe on the counter, she brings them back to the bedroom and places the carafe on the bed stand. One for his head and one for his ankle.

"This is worse than a sprain," she examines him carefully, "you must have fractured it." When he doesn't respond she realizes he has fallen asleep. She stands there staring at him helplessly for a moment, then crosses the cottage and closes the front door, her weariness catching up with her. Lying down next to him, she blows out the lantern and listens to the night until her dreams take over.

The scent of baking bread wakes them. Bright sunlight is streaming through the jalousies into the dusty bedroom, and they are too sore to move from the bed to close them. They have slept into the afternoon, waking now and then to check on each other. As it gets later in the day, they hear someone in the main room clanking things around.

The bloke sits up and looks to the closed bedroom door. "I should see who that is."

"I will do it," the maiden replies, "you can't walk, remember?"

"Right," he says weakly. "But come here first." She hovers over him and they kiss, "be careful."

She steps quietly across the hardwood floor, around the bed, and reaches the door knob. Opening the door just a crack, she sees the fireplace is lit. And standing with her back to the maiden is the white-haired vendor, chopping red bell peppers by a window at the kitchen counter. She turns at the creak of the door.

"You are awake!" The vendor says silkily, excited

to see her. The maiden hesitates, then opens the door all of the way. "I was afraid you would sleep through the meal. Where is your friend?"

Eyeing to room to see if it is safe, she steps forward. "He is hurt. I think he fractured his ankle running from the mob last night."

"Oh no," her hand raises to her chest, "finish cutting these peppers and I will see what I can do." The vendor rushes out the front door into the yard, leaving the maiden where she is standing. Unsure of what to do, she obeys and walks to the kitchen, picking up the knife on the counter.

After a few minutes of chopping the vendor returns with a bag full of ointments and a crutch. Without knocking, she enters the bedroom and sits on the edge of the bed. The bloke starts but she shushes him. "Here darling," she hands him a tonic, "this is for the pain. Drink up." Then pulling up the covers she lightly touches his ankle in several places. "Hmm…" she muses as he winces in pain, "it is broken right here. A hairline fracture. Not bad. It will take some time to heal the break and the sprain."

"How long?" he asks, unable to take his eyes off of her. In the slices of light behind her she is lit like an imprisoned angel. But her voice has a strange drawl to it, like she is leading the listener on to something important. Something secret.

"A few weeks in the least. You damaged the tendons by running on it for so many miles." As she speaks she applies an orange ointment to his skin, rubbing it in. She starts to wrap it with gauze. "Lucky for you I have all of the right things to speed up the process." Finishing the bandage she walks back to the kitchen to inspect the cutting board, leaving the ointments behind for him. "Very good," she says to the maiden. "I need your help with something, come with me."

In the daylight the oak trees look even more

unusual; they surround the cottage like a nest and the bark is so healthy it is almost glowing. The cottage itself has a second floor and a balcony on the porch overhang; it is dressed in vines and moss. She leads her around the side of the house, through a tall hedge. They pass a long, stone table set with beautiful wood-carved dishware and lanterns and are headed for a small shed when she sees it.

The massive trees open up to reveal a towering stone pyramid. Its crumbling foundation reveals its ancient bearing, but it has been well cared for; there are no leaves or vines growing on the structure. The maiden draws breath. There are runes over the doorway and a well worn path leading from it to the shed. The air around it feels still like a sanctuary.

But before she can ask any questions she is back with the vendor, entering the shed. Not without noticing the stares, the vendor hands the maiden a sieve. "All will be explained soon, but first we must tend to the man." She pulls bottles and powders out of cabinets and off of shelves. The shed is full of strange glass objects and herbs. There are plants hanging from the rafters and a smell of burning sage.

She assembles a collection of jars full of grey and tan powders and one of a thick honey colored liquid. Pouring the liquid into a clean container, she ushers the maiden over to her. "Hold this over the E solution. I need to mix these two ingredients with the exact same amount at the exact same time, and you need to shift the sieve evenly until all is mixed." She holds jar containing a powder called Lysine and another called L-arginine in both hands. Pouring them into the sieve, the maiden sifts it obediently. The mix becomes a thick brown concoction that she caps quickly, and rushes away with.

The maiden follows her back into the house where she is promptly instructed to take whatever is baking in the oven out of it so the vendor can tend to the man. She sighs but does as she is told. Within a few minutes the bloke appears at the bedroom door, held up by his crutches with a slightly drunk look on his face. His ankle is tightly wrapped up and he tests the crutches, coming out into the living room.

"She is good!" He says, tripping on the corner of the carpet, "I can't feel a thing." Behind him, the vendor examines her work, and then says, "Wonderful! Now let's eat."

In the back garden they dine on lentil patties covered in roasted peppers with fresh cheese bread. The vendor prepared a peach tea that they sip on silently. Fireflies are popping in and out of view, but the pyramid sits under the oak trees steady and ominous. It has a presence just like any of them and the couple cannot stop staring at it. Finally the vendor breaks the silence.

"I can tell you have many questions," she begins after she is finished eating, "where should we start?"

"Let's start with what the hell happened last night!" the bloke blurts out. "We had the worst timing to be here."

"I agree," she smiles, "unfortunate. But now you are safe, let us remember that."

"Tell us about Samhain," the maiden asks.

The vendor's eyes becomes distant, "The Samhain festival is the most celebrated of all the holidays in the region. It begins the dark half of the year, which unites the autumn equinox with the winter solstice and aligns the lunation with the agricultural cycle of vegetation. This change in season gives the villagers a chance to celebrate a bountiful harvest, and prepare for the most severe season of the year. For winters at this latitude are gruesome and will drive even the thickest-skinned indoors to escape the snow and ice that engulfs the land."

"And the sacrifices?" the bloke inquires.

"The villagers have personified winter into a white

goddess," she takes a sip of her tea, "The White Goddess is said to control the severity of the snowfall, among another things. And so the villagers try to appease her by sacrificing criminals at the stroke of midnight on Samhain - a barbaric practice really. It doesn't make much of a difference to her, how many are sacrificed."

"I thought you said you don't believe in her," the maiden prods.

"Who knows, maybe she is as real as you or me," her eyes linger on the pyramid as she looks between the two, "but the seasons do what they want to. I think she is a myth.

More importantly, I think it is very lucky you two ran into me. Given a few more minutes and they would have had you on your way to the bone-fire. I could see it in their eyes."

The two of them shutter at the idea, and know she is speaking the truth. "Why *did* you help us?" the bloke asks.

"Because I appreciate what the villagers fear in you. You are different from what they have ever seen, different from what I have seen; and the novel is worth saving. And," she opens her arms and wide joyously, "I enjoy company. With your wound you two should be here a while."

The couple exchange unsure looks. But they know she is right. They wouldn't get far without her help. This place is pleasant enough to stay at until he is well. Better here than at the insane town or somewhere alone in the woods. They come to an agreement without saying a word.

"Where were you last night," the maiden asks finally, "when we arrived?"

"Ah, I thought you might ask," she scratches her nose, "I was in there." Her finger aims at the pyramid. They turn around and take it in as she speaks, "It is the safest place on my property, my bedroom, and I wasn't sure you would make it here. We lost each other on the trail and I was afraid. I hid."

"What is it?" the bloke asks.

"I am not sure," she says honestly, "I found it years ago when wandering homeless through this part of the world. It is a special structure. Centuries old. Built by an extinct race of men. There isn't anyone who we *could* ask about it." Her eyes linger on the runes over the door. "I need to ask you both not to disturb the pyramid." Her tone drops lower, "I am doing an ongoing excavation inside and everything is in delicate condition. It would make it easier on my heart if you could respect that one space. Everything else is ours, between the three of us."

"Of course," the maiden agrees, still curious.

"Sure," the bloke answers, "whatever."

The crickets pick up as the sun begins to go down. The vendor stands and begins collecting the dishes. "Why don't we get an early night sleep so we can have a full day tomorrow," she suggests, "I have something to show you both when you wake up."

This sounds like a good idea. They are still tired anyway. Taking the dinnerware back into the cottage, they help the vendor wash the dishes and clean up. Then she bids them goodnight and walks out into the night.

Sinking into bed the bloke takes a big swig of the pain tonic and snuggles into the maiden's hair, wrapping his arms around her waist. He takes a deep breath and starts to sing lightly into her ear;

> When the night came,
> I felt that heaviness,
> Like I always did at dark,
> But we still went for it
> And afterward you filled my broken heart.
> Keep all of your promises
> And when you hit the ground,

Bounce back,
Don't let your life
Be the last thing you expect.

She turns and faces him, placing her hands on his chest, "that is lovely babe. Where did the last part come from? You are the last thing I expected, so it is a good thing."

"I don't know where that came from," he answers, "this tonic makes me feel drunk." She laughs at him. He growls, "I like it, feels good."

"I am turning out the light on you, wounded drunkard!" And she blows out the candle. He grumbles again.

The next day is full of surprises. After a full breakfast of fresh quiche and coffee and cream outside at the stone table, the vendor leads them back into the house and unlocks one of the other doors in the half-circle main room. The carpeted new room is full of musical instruments; harps, guitars, several different-sized drums, a piano, a violin, flutes, and some things the bloke has never seen. He picks up a long wooden tube and examines it.

"That is a Vuvuzela," the vendor says, smiling from the doorway, "it is a horn."

He looks from her stunning face to the goodies in the room and struggles to say, "This is amazing." Hobbling over to a chair he picks up a guitar and gives it a strum. "I haven't held one of these in months."

"Well go ahead," she encourages. The maiden sits on the carpet to listen, and he faces her and starts to play a song he has been forming in his head for weeks;

"Do you think you inspire me?
Is it because you desire me?
This song is overdue and I sing it to you.

You are the coals to this flame.
It is in the way you say my name.
My name now belongs to you.
If I said you are amazing
I'm being lazy
with my words.
You are the coals to this flame.
It is in the way you say my name.
My name now belongs to you."

When he finishes the last strum, the maiden sighs. "Babe, I love it!" she croons. Glowing, she stands up and embraces him, planting her lips on his in a slow kiss. The vendor claps her hands enthusiastically and looks at the two of them in wonder. They have a special energy between them, this is obvious. The way they open themselves up to each other makes the room expand. It is the most beautiful thing she has ever seen. Her wide eyes aren't missed by the bloke.

"Play us something!" he insists, curious of her intent.

She laughs nervously for the first time, "I can't play." The maiden is shocked and openly gawks at her. "Music is the most ethereal thing in the world," she beings, "but I can't make it myself." Her head sinks, as if she is ashamed for owning so much of what she doesn't have. These dusty instruments are a testament of a talent she has never possessed but has coveted since she heard her first psalms. She crosses the room and idly tinkers a few notes on the piano, "it is a part of the soul that sends vibrations the farthest. Images are one thing, but music! You can appreciate it in your sleep! And the lyrics! The words of a musician, they are hypnotizing. The best songs are repetitive and you become them. You become the musician," she focuses on the bloke, "but not really. Because it isn't possible for me to replicate."

The sincerity of her high tone causes the deepest sympathy. Her veil of mystery drops for a moment and she is a creature unsatisfied with her countenance. Frail even. The striking pale skin and exotically asymmetrical features on her face seem to accept all that she is in full for a fleeting moment. Large blue eyes slightly far apart with a delicate nose and full burgundy lips; the body of a tall, small-waisted, gangly beauty. She is powerful and wise, yet incomplete somehow.

"Have you ever tried," the maiden begins, "with a teacher?"

"Have you!" she gets defensive suddenly. Her eyes darken.

" Uh, well yes," she starts.

"You have?!" the bloke turns to her in surprise.

"Yes, haven't I told you? Classical music, but that isn't the point." She faces him, "why don't you teach her?"

The possibility crosses the room. A professional sizes up the endless supply of equipment and what seems to be a ready pupil. The owner feels like she could perhaps open up in this situation, being that she will gain something worth a hundred deaths. They consider each other, and then the vendor says, "We will start tomorrow morning. Stay here and practice." Extending her hand to the maiden, she says, "I have something to show *you* now."

Happy about the arrangement, she takes her hand and follows the vendor into the half moon living room. Directly to the right of the fireplace there is a thin door that she deftly unlocks and opens. A narrow spiral staircase loops up out of view, and she mounts the steps knowing the maiden will be right behind her. At the top of the stair she unlocks a second door and lets it swing open.

In the light of the top story window, the circular room is crowned with a golden bar that holds countless dazzling garments; floor-length silk gowns, couture fleeces, lace turtleneck throw-overs and satin tops. By the window, a vanity sits under glittering necklaces and ornate rings hang from an expansive crystal antler. There is a round swivel stand in the middle of the floor which holds scores of high heeled shoes, hats, gloves, feathers, and medallions. And on the wall there is a shelf full of bottled lotions, creams, powders and balms.

The maiden steps into the room and runs her hands across a velvet dress, taking it all in. The wardrobe room probably took many years to fill, considering the grandeur of the gowns and the expense it would take to import them here. It seems so impossible that they are here at all. Then remembering the humble garb worn by the vendor, the sight of the clothes becomes even more perplexing.

"Impressive," is all she can find to say. "Where do you wear these?"

"I don't," the vendor answers simply, "there is nowhere to wear them. But as I told you at the market, I collect beautiful things. While you are here you are welcome to wear whatever you like."

"I um," the maiden sets down a veiled hat, "I haven't dressed in anything grand since I stopped dancing. I don't know where I would begin. And I would feel silly wearing gowns in the forest, like some kind of elf," she laughs, "dressing fabulously without a point-"

"You don't need a purpose to look your best. Do it because you love it." The vendor takes a tortuous shell comb and forks it into the maiden's thick hair. "But it so happens, you do have reason for dressing up." She passes the vanity and opens a door to the right.

The second story wardrobe room gives way to the balcony that covers the porch. The height allows for a breathtaking view of the downward sloping forest. Everything is alive and swaying with the yellows and oranges of fall, and beyond is a distant view of a great green lake. It also offers a confronting view of the face of the stone pyramid, which sits under shady oak.

Against the banister is a squash, red velvet cushion, and before that, an easel is set up with a blank canvas waiting for decoration. The vendor set out about a hundred bottles of open paint cans and there are brushes littering the deck.

"Painting is my truest gift, and it is truly a work of the fates when my friends happen to be such beautiful subjects."

"You want to paint me?" the maiden asks.

"My portfolio is dull, and I cannot paint another landscape. With your image added to it I may be able to make it into the national gallery! Go and chose an outfit while I prime the canvas. This is going to be great!"

The days pass this way, between music lessons, tea, delicious meals, costume design and painting; they have no end of entertaining themselves. The autumn leaves stay late on the tall oak, some come to rest on the courtyard floor, but to the three, time seems not to pass at all. They treat each other with respect and courtesy; the vendor constantly inventing a new way to amuse themselves, the maiden appearing lovely and elaborately adorned now in all occasions, and the bloke writing new music as it comes to him frequently. They come to appreciate each other's quirks and habits more than their own, and spend the long, cool nights discussing what they believe of the world, how it works and their own unique purposes as they try to define them.

One day, after spending time in deep thought, the vendor approaches them with an idea. Explaining now that their time together is more precious than she could have imagined, she suggests they each plant a vine on the side of the cottage. Three star jasmine vines that can grow from thin, individual vines into a full, blossoming, climbing bush that she desires to adorn the house. The couple finds this to be a charming idea and are touched at how important they have become to her. They spend an afternoon digging deep holes and carefully placing their budding vines side by side. As they grow, the vendor is pleased to see that they are indeed intertwining, must faster than she anticipated.

They have so much growth to show for their pastimes. The bloke, listening to the soothing voice of the vendor practice her lessons, begins using her words in his songs during their private tutoring. Just small diddles about the way a healer thinks, and how all animals on earth should share their love. He keeps these to himself, and during their evenings on the balcony, he plays the more familiar ones the maiden loves while she focuses on finding an attractive pose for the vendor to paint; the maiden's favorite songs are the ones where he swears his devotion to her. And the maiden spends her hours upstairs admiring the way the dresses fit her blossoming body and practicing poses for the vendor to capture in the vanity.

The flat wall in the half-moon living room is quickly losing free space as it is covered daily by drying oil paintings of the beautiful redhead in different costumes - dancing as a ballerina, sprinting through the dark forest as a sprite, lounging on the red velvet cushion - whatever they imagine together comes to life with her practiced hand. And the maiden is always delighted at the creative scenarios the vendor establishes for her to play.

Their play becomes more real to them than their previous reality. It has layers they invent for themselves. The sanctuary holds them safe with all they could possibly want and need and their past lives seem unimportant compared to the endless indulgence they have come to love. Around the fire place they make up stories together and mold themselves into the characters. The maiden plays a nun, the bloke plays God, and the vendor plays an evil spirit. Then they switch roles for fun and are surprised at how easily they fill it.

Even their dreams take a turn at night. Holding

each other in their bedroom, the bloke will dream that he is becoming an angel of light, just as he has always wanted to be while the maiden has ghastly dreams that she is growing black wings and has sharp three-inch fingernails. Asleep under the pointed, lightning laced roof of the pyramid, the vendor becomes more alive in her dreams of perfectly balanced scales and intertwining jasmine vines.

One evening after they have finished a card game under the lantern lit front porch, they sit enjoying the gentle hues of the darkening sky blues when the vendor opens up a subject they haven't discussed. They have exhausted science, politics, religion, and world travel. Now she asks them individually what they desire more than anything in the world. After a pause that allows for the owls to speak, the bloke goes first.

"More than anything," he says, gazing at the sky, "I want to know what is beyond this illusion. I want to know the truth, the real truth about why we exist. That is why I am here, with you two anyway. Hoping to find some new way that truth can manifest."

His thoughts settle in their ears, and the vendor asks, "What do you think you have discovered so far?"

"I think I am learning more about the laws of attraction. How the positive and the negative can attract each other. It is insane how we got here. The things that happened in the village that led us to be here. It is like the negative attracts the positive, or vice versa."

"Opposites attract," the vendor smiles. "Opposite doesn't necessarily mean negative. And, if there were no illusion, there would be no enlightenment. If we are here to enable the divine purpose of the universe to unfold, then the divine purpose of the universe to unfold is to enable us. It makes things symmetrical."

"Yes, and it is the unity between them that I want," he says, "the balance. I think you understand!"

"Everything is calculated subconsciously," she

continues in a sort of rhythm. "We follow our hearts that leads our minds to calculate the breeds. Behind our shadows arise perfect space and time, and after time we live to get by. But where are we going when we pass through lies? Are we entering our passwords in truth? Truth is the forbidden fruit."

The maiden claps her hands in surprise. "Bravo! I was wondering when you would start sharing your rhymes with me too."

The vendor's cheeks flush with pleasure, "the opportunities are arising. In the sense that the applications of the knowledge attained can be put to practice now. The simple life of loving humanity shines bright in the oak forest!" They both cheer. "The truth for me is, I have been left to fend for myself for so long. I got stopped over and over again only to know that what I was experiencing was preparing me for something. That means that it was real. Which leads me to believe that everything here, now with you is real. Love is real!"

They listen, slightly shocked at her openness, "Oh boy it's real! I used to spend all of my time in the villages, but virtually alone. I thought close human contact was debasing. But now my sight is back and I barely remember that time. For the first time ever in our known history we can appreciate the idea of peaceful existence among humans."

This goes over the couple's heads, but they are too excited to hear her heart, so they don't interrupt. "Why were we told to be scared? What I want more than anything in the world right now is this: love, singularity and community! We are supposed to live in groups. It is good for the heart. Humans are not self-sustaining; they are open-looped and need each other to regulate one another in a harmonious balance. We are doing it. We are building a community. We are doing what needs to be done! We are creating an alliance! We support each other! We are the evolution! We are the connection! We are the action!"

She stands up and paces a few steps, lost in thought. Her eyes bright and glowing, almost forgetting they are there. In all her life she has never known such openness with humans. They aren't vile and as far beneath her as she has been taught to think. They are clever, and kind, and their depth makes her feel the most amazing acceptance she has ever felt. The love they have for each other that is now spreading to her is intoxicating. She feels powerfully real.

How do you get someone to do what you want them to? How do you get them to move, to stay? In a positive way? How does she change her habits to protect the love and not destroy it? To spread it. You make art. You lead them to see. You let them feel, let them decide. You let your ego rest for a moment and be real.

Her head is spinning and she imagines how she will present this to the Southern Summit. They will never accept it, probably never believe it. She must protect it now and worry about that when the time comes. Noticing their alarm at her silent pacing, she places herself back into a chair and clears her throat. Opening her mouth to speak, a laugh breaks out. Then she doubles over, laughing so ecstatic it is uncontrollable.

Then the bloke starts laughing, and the maiden joins in. They all find it amusing and their joy echoes through the night ending with a collective sigh. Collecting herself, the vendor finally turns to the maiden and asks what *she* wants more than anything in the world.

Before she responds, she considers so many possible answers. The bloke has had time to think on this for ten years longer than she has, and the vendor, acting out of passion, could speak her mind clearly and honestly. But what does she want? The wants are subject to change from moment to moment; an unstable pursuit. If she were to say what she wanted a few weeks ago, it would have to be freedom from the guilt of leaving her family the way she did; running off into the night with stolen cherished family heirlooms. If she were to look at what she wanted after she met the bloke, it would to be free to love him fully by letting go of herself, which she struggles to do all the time. If she were to look at what she is seeing right now, it would be to be free of the hesitance she has in trusting the safety of this situation.

She looks at her hands and thinks of what they are capable of, the potential they have to manifest the powerful feelings she is struggling with. Being with the two of them in isolation for so long, while watching them build things from their imaginations, something she envies yet knows she is capable of doing, is adding to a frustration she has always had. To know who she is and what she can do. What kind of art can she make? The dancing she did so long ago was choreographed by another person; it was made for her, yes, but made by someone else. So far she has only been the vessel they use to make their projects; their paintings and their songs. And while that makes her feel special beyond expression, she has something she is unable to express. Has the lack of inner freedom to express. Speaking more to herself than to the others she says…

"I want to be free." She waits for an objection, and when neither interrupts, she clarifies, "I want freedom."

The two linger on the idea of freedom to themselves for a moment, and then the bloke says simply, "We can help with that."

"If you want to be free," the vendor adds in, "quiet the voice in your head. Listen to me. I can teach you how to cast spells that will enable your freedom."

"Spells?" the maiden asks.

"I really want to help you. To train you. Training is communication. Training is healing. But you have to be careful with what you ask for. Ask for freedom to yourself every night. Write it down, the exact words of what you want to be free from - spell it out. Ask and you will receive."

    The next morning the sky is overcast, the wind promises rain and a drop in the temperature. In the early hours the maiden quietly climbs the spiral staircase to the wardrobe room upstairs and places herself in the chair before the vanity. The light hasn't quite lit the room bright enough for her to see all of her features, so she waits, and she watches.

    For the first half of an hour she stares into the backward world of the mirror. She has spent many hours in front of this vanity, but today, for once, she sees more than just her familiar reflection staring back at her. Though she doesn't know what she is wrestling with, she whispers for it to show her freedom. On a piece of paper, she spells out the seven-letter word.

    This vertical pool of glass appears to be a portal into a different place in time. The mechanics are simple enough. With her naked eye she can almost see the trillions of streaming photons bounce off of the smooth glass. She leans in closer and feels the warm light waves slide through liquid sand, hit the reflective silver layer painted on the back of the mirror, and shoot back at her in every direction at once; only a few million of these make it into her eyes where they are perceived and acknowledged. The rest zoom away to some place she will never know.

    Her brown irises tighten around their pupils as the light penetrates the protective cornea. They bend and flip through the lenses and hit the retina in the far cavern in the back of her eyes where the little rod cells detect the intensity of the sunlight from the window behind her vanity and the cone cells tell her that her lacey bra is indeed purple. Together those rods and cones meet with their cell friend ganglion, and they pass along a secret message through each synapse in a game of telephone till it reaches the occipital lobe of her brain. And finally, after she has already moved and the atoms and molecules have changed from their original position, the telephoned message is decoded and a lovely, time displaced, image is produced; and there she is in reflection.

But is this a portal into the future, the present or the past? All the encrypted talk between the bloke and the vendor about illusions has provoked her to look harder at her world. Because, at the present moment she is eye-to-glass with the mirror, searching to see her physical body in the immediate *now*. She looks to the right and her reflection looks to its left. It does exactly what she does at seemingly the same rate creating an illusion of synchronicity; but by the time the maiden's brain registers what she sees, enough milliseconds have passed to where dozens of cells may have divided into two or randomly died, altering her physical appearance before she can ever see it as it is. She realizes she is always looking at a delayed version of herself.

Can this be a part of the illusion they spoke of? A world of images that are perceived at a time that isn't linear and is relevant only to the viewer? What if that world inside the mirror, the backward one, is the real world and the one she is in is the illusion. What if she is backward!

Suddenly she understands why she, herself in her body could be an illusion. She has no need to be so possessive of it. Is this the answer to freedom she was asking for?

Downstairs in the bedroom the bloke stirs. It is still so early that no light is shining through the jalousies. He would go back to sleep if only his ankle did not ache so much. Taking a swig of the tonic, he eases up and dresses not even noticing his bedmate is missing.

In the bathroom, he can't help but be drawn to a rusted mirror hanging over the sink. Shaking his body to clear his head, he takes a strong look at himself just to be sure of whom he is.

What appears to be the reflection of a 28-year-old man standing alone in the bathroom is in fact much more. He holds up his hand, waves to himself and then smiles. For the first time he sees that he is not alone at all. He is completely and incomprehensibly tied to the entire world around him; and always has been despite his former beliefs that he is the center of it all. Suddenly a burning thought reaches his mind. He *is* the balance, but there is more.

He heads to the music room and snatches the guitar off of the carpet. Something inside him is churning, but he can't identify it. So he plays it out on the guitar strings. A beautiful, complicated three-part song in ¾ time. Absorbed in the melody, he doesn't notice someone else enter the room.

"I can't help but observe how well you capture people in your songs - situations even." The vendor glides around the room and leans against the piano gazing at him in a long, unbroken assessment. "Especially when it comes to the maiden, you use her well."

"She is my muse. A muse in general. She helps my musing," he coughs.

"Using, musing, it is all the same. The girl lives in a world of thought, still trying to determine who she is. You live in a world of action. That makes you very powerful, you know. Action outweighs thought because action is thought to its fullest potential. Thought is an unfinished action, while action is a finished thought."

He thinks this over and she licks her lips, continuing, "She will not be able to manifest her thoughts while you have power over her. Not without outside help. She will leave. That is just a thought, anyway."

Her words stir that questionable feeling he has inside him, and he doesn't know how to respond. There is truth in what she says. Tinkering a few notes on the piano as she usually does she heads toward the door. Pausing just under the frame, she leans against it, "You know, your song writing has more potential than you give it. Feel out for different wills, a more mature will. You have more available to you than you realize." Her body slinks out into the half-moon living room and up the spiral staircase leaving him to consider what she is proposing.

They move quickly down the path behind the pyramid that stretches down the sloping forest into the darkening gloom. Barefoot, the vendor skips happily just ahead of the maiden, who is content to get away from the property for the late morning. Just after parting ways with the bloke in the music room, the vendor invited the maiden to a girl's day out, suggesting another surprise is in store.

After refusing to answer the maiden's inquiries, the path slopes down into a rocky, leaf-layered terrain. The texture of the rock is strangely familiar to the maiden. And then the trees open up to a steep cliff that juts down to a small, crystal-blue pond, and the boughs creating a kind of branch-like roof. Somehow, the pond is clear of leaves. The water seems to resonate a peaceful vibration. The rock at the bottom appears to have been scraped up, but is so deep that it is a dark sapphire blue.

"This," the vendor begins, "is what I believe to be the limestone quarry that was made during the construction of the pyramid. Look, see the cube-like indentions? This is a sacred place. Let's sit on the edge and listen to the water."

On a small ledge, they assume a cross legged position and let the silence seep into them. Something like the feeling she connected with in front of the looking glass comes over the maiden. Like a kind of disconnected freedom one finds in a trance.

"I want you to know something," the vendor starts. "Life never rejects, it directs. Follow the light that guides; what humans call our hearts. This is something you must understand about being a woman. You hold an intuitive key to the unraveling of the fabric of time. Your friend, he fears this in you. He fears the divine femininity."

"What is there to fear? I don't understand," the maiden asks.

"A woman is the womb. She is life. Something a man can never create on his own."

"Women cannot create it on their own either."

"But women are more evolved, and are evolving faster. Some female sharks can reproduce asexually - they don't need males."

"So you think he is afraid that I will run off and impregnate myself by myself?"

"Don't be cheeky," the vendor laughs, "your man is more intuitive than most. He can sense something evolving in you. To infinity we exist in multiple dimensions!"

"What does this mean?"

"Each person's perception is a new dimension, and there are an infinite amount of dimensions curled up in space that rotate, spin, and bond all at once! He had never allowed himself to blend his dimension with another person's dimension; he was so absorbed in his own sphere, this being God thing, that he didn't even know it was possible. Only now is he opening up to the possibility of a larger conglomerate."

"I don't know," the maiden wonders, "I feel like our dimensions have opened to each other..."

"But it can be so much bigger. Don't you see that this is what happens when stars collide!" When the maiden doesn't respond enthusiastically, the vendor vents, "It seems like you have been trained to kneel, sit, and beg at the foot of your masters."

"What, him?"

"To every human. It seems as though this is a skill you developed to protect yourself from danger and control your environment. Know this. I come in peace. I will never harm you. No one ever will while you are here. You are safe always. Trust in love. Trust in respect. Trust in me, because as we spend more days together, I am you and you are me and we are here with each other through eternity. So we might as well get this out of the way so we can move on to the cool stuff. Like this!"

And she steps closer to the edge, pulls her dress over her head so that she is standing naked, her stark white body brilliant against the blue behind her. With a big smile to the maiden, and a yelp, she turns around and jumps off of the edge and falls the fifteen feet, splashing into the pool. The maiden cries and rushes to the ledge to look below. Splashing around in a circle, the vendor waves her down, "Come in!"

"What! Naked? No way!"

"The water feels amazing."

"I am sure it does, I can appreciate it from here."

"Come on! You said you wanted freedom!"

"You are trying to manipulate me!"

"Only a little," she laughs, "Trust me! You will love this."

"No way."

"Let go!"

"No"

"Yes!"

"NO!"

"Let go!"

The maiden takes a deep breath, feels a spike of adrenaline, and backs away from the edge into the trees. She peels off her dress looking over her shoulders, and when she builds up the courage, completely naked; she runs full speed off of the cliff. The free fall seems to go in slow motion with the surface of the lake coming at her like a bubble. Then she breaks the surface and sinks under. The water is warmer than the air and has a mineral taste that feels just as good as it looks and the vendor is laughing her face off, struggling to stay afloat. "Beautiful," she spits out water, "that was beautiful." She swims over and kisses her quickly on the mouth. The maiden, surprised, bursts out laughing and kisses her on the cheek.

They splash each other and do laps as the clouds overhead darken until the sky begins to shower on them. Speeding to navigate up the cliff before the rain falls too heavy, they climb over the crest and struggle their dresses back on. The maiden is still giddy to be so exposed. It isn't long before their dresses drag through the gathering mud and they break out into a run before they lose all visibility. The maiden's hands begin to freeze and she tucks them into fists, but the cold earth is weeping with a winter's first accomplishment, and the chill creeps into her very bones. The vendor doesn't seem to notice this or be bothered by the chill at all. She runs freely, with a smile still in her eyes.

"You know that journal you keep with you?" She calls back to the panting maiden, "You read it a lot?"

"Yea," she struggles to say.

"Maybe that is your calling. Maybe you are meant to write, like she did."

The maiden is too tired to respond. They come sloshing into view of the streaming pyramid, around the courtyard, and straight into the shed. The vendor gives the maiden a vile of powder to take to rid her of the chill, and then they walk around, into the house to start the fireplace.

"Where have you been?" the bloke crutches into the room, taking in their wet appearance.

"Hold on love, I need to change before I become an icicle," the maiden dashes up the spiral staircase, out of sight.

"Wow," the vendor sighs from the cushion. *"That* was real."

"What was?"

"You and I both know each other," her voice lowers, "can you feel what I am feeling?"

"What did you two do today?" he asks suspiciously. "I got a kiss."

For a second, he doesn't know what to say. A pain of jealousy stabs him. Then a curious feeling comes over him and the bloke shares her smile, "you girls…" he playfully chides.

That evening the maiden comes down with a cold. She excuses herself to stay in bed with a handkerchief, tonic, a pen and paper. The patter from the rain makes a barrier of sound, and so none of the residents can hear what the other is doing. Taking advantage of this they each go about their own art.

Across a sheet of rain and the courtyard, the vendor is on the brink of a discovery. After consulting *Humans and Synchronicity,* she is aware that the formations of White Powder Gold are subject to change over time. Slightly feverish with excitement, she takes a pinch of the powder into her fist, squeezes it three times, and blows it over the flame on the candlestick on the edge of her bed. The dust whirls through the air in a cloud, and then zooms into the wall facing the house. She brings the candle right up to the symbol just to be sure, then she feels a bubble of joy inside her explode and she laughs a melodic laugh mingled with a sigh of satisfaction. The formation on the wall is no longer a circle, but that of a perfect triangle.

"A pyramid," she whispers.

Still in shock, she cannot decide what she needs to do. She fumbles around, almost dropping her candle until she finds her gold coin marked X across the face, and Y across the emblem of the village clock tower. Before she flips it, she already knows what it will land on. It clinks onto the limestone floor with a large X reading back at her.

In the music room, the bloke struggles over a few lines of a chorus he gave up on an hour ago. There are papers strewn across the carpet, several wadded up and torn, most of them filled with writing that looks more like letters to oneself than a page of lyrics. The words "I got enough friends, friends indeed, I don't want to get to know you or your personality," face him as a part of an unfinished song, but most of what he has written are thoughts that have gone horribly wrong. A warm presence behind him alerts him to what he has been waiting up for.

She stands in her usual spot, leaning her back against the door frame. Her body is draped in a free flowing copper mesh dress embroidered with tiny pearl vines that hug every curve leaving little to the imagination, and she is humming an off key, but guttural low pitched tune; her feet are bare. Her gaze is not in her usual intimidating stare down, instead it roams the floor, taking in the mess he has made, and ends with staring at the core of his body.

He fights the urge to cross his chest. "I am sorry about the chaos I have created in here," he tries to throw her attention to the room. She isn't taking the bait.

"What we think is chaos is often more organized than we can understand at the point it is made." The vendor hasn't stopped staring at his chest and he does not know what to say to fill the space between them, which seems to be disappearing without either of them needing to move.

"I want to show you something," she flicks her head back, her hair dancing around her face, "Come with me."

A sheet of icy rain greets them at the front door. She drapes a rain poncho over his head and pulls it down over his body, he can hardly move, and covering herself with a second one, she takes his hand firmly and they close the door behind him, letting the rain fill the space between them and the cottage. Around the puddles in the courtyard he is shocked to see where she is taking him. Though the night drapes the forest in darkness, the pyramid has a light glow emanating from within. Its light lives inside the very stones it is made of.

He finds he is holding his breath when they approach the stone door. She pushes hard and the stone starts to give, but she turns to him and demands him to close his eyes before she will go any further. Shutting out the world, he follows her lead into the surprisingly warm chamber. She tells him to stand still and then closes out the rain. The chamber sounds like it is buzzing, and a strange lightning crosses the red of this eye lids. Perplexed he doesn't hear her walk around him.

"Open your eyes."

It is as if the ceiling is attacking him, he drops to the floor and instinctively covers his head. The chamber is filled with dazzling electric lights that buzz and gently work their way down a bed frame that lay in the center of the floor and into the vendor's skin. If he didn't know better he would think she is being electrocuted; but the light makes her more alive, as if her skin cells want to do front flips.

"What do you think of my bedroom?" He is unable to respond, "amazing isn't it? I can see you know it is working its magic on me. Keeping me alive."

Her white hair stands on end and her eyes are dilated, yet as icy as the rain that falls outside. No one could be so perfect as this. No human. The way she glides to the edge of the bed, almost floating, to take his hand and invite him in, the closer he is to her, the more weightless she becomes. They stand on their knees, face to face. The electricity sparking the air between them, and latching onto his skin, sinking in like a drug.

"What is this? What are you?" He watches the lines on his hands fade away. He is terrified - thrilled - but cannot move.

"Don't you see? *I* am the darkness, *she* is the light, and *you* are the balance; a pyramid. Can you feel this happening? We are meant to be together, the three of us, to connect. Connect! Look!!" A few chunks of her shoulder length white hair turns gold. She is becoming so stunning it is hard for him to look at her. Before he can break the connection she stares deep into his eyes, "make love to me. Make love to my mind."

That is all he needed to hear. He lunges forward and pulls her dress over her head.

Ink fills page after page of a personal notebook in a sick room occupied for several days now. As regular as the rainfall, the secondary relationship intensifies in the pyramid, and when there are free moments, the vendor spends time with the maiden, who admires the former's new hair color with a weak voice as she drinks down the bitter tonic so generously offered. The sniffing young woman, who hasn't been able to hold any sustenance down, cannot thank her host enough for her insight into writing. Her scribbled thoughts have been her only distraction from the cough that racks her throat and the vomit bucket beside the bed; which is why she quarantines herself away. Encouraged by her friend, she lets her feelings run freely, sometimes without real form, onto the paper; feeling mostly for her lover, and secondly for the trust in a new friend. The vendor is openly delighted and giggles loudly when she reads the rough poems and beginnings of short stories; adding cheery laughter between moans of pain. Acting on the vendor's idea, she keeps her writing to her friends critique only, as a surprise to her love.

The bloke has taken a second bedroom to avoid the sickness, which the vendor has described to be something they as outsiders do not have immunity to. It is not safe for him to visit her while the virus is active. So he watches helplessly while the vendor blows him a kiss behind her shoulder before closing the bedroom door to the sick room. His mind's eye is active with thoughts of the vendor's seduction; he cannot help but think that she and the maiden have been up to something more than healing behind that closed door. Sometimes he strains to listen over the patter of the rain and hears the maiden's familiar moan accompanied by a squeal of joy and intimate laughter. He once heard the vendor shout out, "that is SO GOOD!" in a way that almost provoked him to rush to the door.

But he thought better of it. So what if they are sharing a bed together. Maybe the red-head is looking for new ways to manifest her feelings. She did ask for freedom didn't she?

When the secondary couple is not making love in the pyramid, which occupies most of their daytime activity, or when the vendor is caring for the maiden, his foot now healed from the pyramid, the bloke explores every crack of the cottage. Able to climb the stairs now, he has spent many of the mind-unhinging rainy days in the wardrobe room, picking his guitar, trying to pass the time. He itches to be outside, to be downstairs in the bedroom with the women, to be anywhere but in limbo land. So he writes page after page of frustrated lyrics, letting the that familiar darkness creep over him and influence his words. If he has the light and the dark to pull from, what does the light look like in the shade? He paces the floor and gazes out of the window, watching the pyramid cry in the rain, writing down what his dichotomies tell him. Nothing is sacred anymore.

One evening, while doing just this, waiting for the women to be done with each other, something from his gut tugs at him. He paces the floor again, thinking to himself. The maiden is the light, and the vendor is the dark. He is the balance. But *why* is the vendor the dark? Aside from being manipulative, which most females are, how has she come to identify herself as a dark being? Especially seeing that her pyramid gives off a brilliant light and the fact that she has helped them so much. That doesn't seem dark to him. And if it takes all three of them for the pyramid to work, they must be doing something right. But something doesn't sit right with him, still. The answer lies within the pyramid. It must! With absolution, he heads for the spiral staircase determined to investigate, leaving his papers all over the wardrobe room floor.

But as he lands into the half-moon living room, he is surprised to see the maiden on the couch by the fireplace, sharing a blanket and a laugh with the vendor. The two of them hush whatever they were talking about before he entered and share a secret smile. "There you are my love!" She reaches her hand out, her face is pale and thin, but she wears a weary glow.

"Hi," he looks past her hand and pretends to fumble with the poncho in his hand.

"Going somewhere?" the vendor eyes his gear.

"I was just, putting this away."

The room is silent. The maiden, weakened as she is draws back into the vendor's shoulder at his rejection. He grunts to himself and stiffly walks past the two of them, pausing by the door. And before he goes in, he says spitefully, "I will leave you two to your *girly* things. Unless I can watch."

The vendor raises her eyebrow, and the maiden crosses her arms defensively. Hurt by the tone of his voice she feels he is belittling her; the maiden is protective over the poem she was just perfecting with her friend.

"Like you let me watch when you are with her?" she says sitting up taller. "You never let me do anything!"

So she does know, the bloke thinks. He bristles, "You are such a little girl. When you grow up, maybe we will let you join in."

"That is what I wanted from the beginning! Always!"

"Liar!"

"I can't believe you!"

"This could work if you weren't such a sneaky

liar!"

"Calm down you two!" the vendor shouts over them. It shuts their mouths, but they glare as if it is the first time they have seen each other. "Sit!" she points to a bean bag on the floor, and the bloke plants himself into it. She squeezes the maiden's arm reassuringly and then edges around a table and positions herself behind him. Resting her hands on his shoulders, she starts to massage his tense muscles with heavy strokes. The maiden's eyes grow wide as she sees how easily he forms to her touch. So easy it is uneasy.

"Sharing is caring, dears. Share love. You must share love."

Watching him bend at her will makes the maiden's stomach churn. It is all she can do to keep her heart from imploding, but she cannot take her eyes off of what she thinks she is witnessing. She cannot move. His eyes roll up in pleasure and his mouth drops open. When he lets out a small moan the maiden stands to her feet and wobbles to her sick room.

Regretfully, he brushes the vendor's hand away and follows her just to the door. Her face is paler than a white rose, and all he can say is, "I am sorry. I truly am." And she can't help but kiss him softly in acceptance and submission before pulling away. She closes the door and listens to the vendor reassure the bloke in quiet whispers, saying something about protecting the pyramid, and then excusing herself to the shed. The bloke creaks the front door open after she is well gone, and vanishes into the rain on some personal errand.

Wide awake in the night, the maiden forces her muscles to move out of the warm down blankets. The cold floors send a chill down her spine and she imagines the fleece coats and fur socks upstairs in the wardrobe room. She will need them if she wants to make a snack

comfortably in the kitchen. Tip toeing up the stairs, she is
sure she will not be heard by the empty house.

Under the lamplight, the room is different than how
she left it. The bloke's mess is everywhere; leftover,
spoiled food, incense ash on every surface he could use,
and scraps of notebook paper litter the floor every
direction. With a heavy sigh, she ambles around the piles
for the sock drawer on the far side of the round table.
Wobbling slightly as she kneels to open it, something on
the floor catches her eye. The air becomes still outside, and
in the room. A torn sheet of paper lies face up. She can't
help to want to know what he has been thinking, and when
the candle lights it, she reads;

"When the sun goes down and emotions come out,
And your wood inlayed eyes keep staring at the ground.
Mission accomplished,
Do you feel regret burning down your neck?
Broken friendships in progress.
Do you ever wonder why your soul is in debt?"
You are just a body and a slave to me.
If I never saw you again I wouldn't miss a beat.
So shut your mouth we are going to do it my way,
Tie you up to give you pleasure and pain.
And if you don't want to play
It isn't the end.
I have other ways.
I will just take your friend."

She freezes in place. There is more, but she cannot
read it. The urge to vomit strikes her again, and she suffers
a small cry, holding it in. She casts the candle light over
the floor and all she sees are words attacking her, loving
her, hating her, missing her, cursing her; the ramblings of a
two-sided personality directing his inner turmoil right at her
heart.

123

Taking a black, fur-lined coat from the rack and donning a pair of thick boots, she inhales as much bravery as she can find. There is only one reason she can think of that could cause his love to turn to hate so quickly; guilt. And the crimes he may have committed… her suspicions feel like a burning poison eating out her insides. But she has to know.

The thick mud is already crystallizing and she crashes through the thin ice in a fury. Winter's white kiss threatens the world below; the rain clouds have retreated high up and have turned a pale grey, contrasting with the impenetrable shade under the trees. There is no moon tonight. The path is covered quickly without thought, and there before her is the tall hallow pyramid, emitting it's sickening glow.

The perforated stone door is her only barrier and it has no handle. Without thinking she pulls back and throws her weight into the stone, scraping her shoulder and seeing stars in her weariness, but it gives just enough to know she made the right choice. She crashes into it again and again, biting her lip to quench the pain until it is wide enough for her to fit, she slides through the gap, finding herself immersed in lightning.

Lights fly everywhere, around and through her and she grips the slanted wall, trying to focus on any solid she can find. Her eyes go to the point in the ceiling where the light is concentrated and follows the thickest beam down, down to where there are two figures, whitest of everything, intertwined. Their naked bodies joined together, focused on each other, it is shockingly real. Jolted by the sight, she impulsively runs forward to separate what she sees only to have the lighting intensify and blind her vision, threads of it break off and attach to her skin, pulling her forward to the light. Her body grows lighter and is starting to lift off of the floor, drawn to the center. And then she gathers all of her will and screams.

"NO!!!"

The lights dim. Pulling away from each other slowly, they are not surprised to see her. The bloke covers himself in a slight attempt at modesty, but the vendor opens her arms wide in reception, ignoring the hurt she reads on her face. The maiden quails and the lights in the ceiling dim even more. The vendor notices this and shows doubt for the first time.

Speechless, the maiden cannot think, she can barely stand. The bloke is the first to voice his angst, "Well, what did you expect? It can go both ways. Sharing is caring."

"Sharing!?"

"I can see right through you and all of your facades. Someday you will understand when you are honest with yourself. You are honest with everyone else so let your walls come crumbling down. Your soul is what you face, and that you have found."

"This is what you meant by sharing? Is this what this was all about, the whole time?!"

"You are such a know-it-all. But you don't know the way I fall. Now you have set it off. Take a look in the mirror, that is all you are thinking about." He grabs his clothes and hastily throws them on, "Know it all! Know it all! You've hit the floor. You have sold your soul to yourself, out of control. And you don't know what is right anymore."

"You told me I could count on you but you won't let me count you!!" the maiden cries.

"I see your ugly face and it ostracizes you. There is no chance I could ever love you. A thousand makeovers could not pardon your appearance. You are vain. Let the killers kill you. Let the vultures take you away. This space is not compatible for the both of us. Count me out." He stands firm and doesn't leave the vendor's side.

Like a knife cutting flesh in half, their bond tears

with his words. Both of them feel the burn and shrink in stature. The light above pinches out, leaving only a small red glow. Then vendor grabs the bedpost for support, gasping for air.

"Have you nothing to say for yourself you witch!?" The maiden yells at her.

The vendor's hair has retreated to white again, and her hands are wrinkling before their very eyes. Then the bloke finally feels that thing in his gut settle. That nagging question about light and darkness. She is the darkness because she is-

"The White Goddess! You are the White Goddess!" he laughs hysterically, "this place will go down in history!"

Holding onto the bed frame with both hands, she raises her head to meet the maidens eyes. The wasteful years of evil spurning surface on those once beautiful features, now a melting mask of pitiful desperation. One good look at the witch's deteriorating skin and the heart sick turns to an urge to flee. A memory of the upside down woman's gaping face in the hands of the mob, and her submission to a hopeless death at the sight of the vendor's hair pen sweeps by. All of those people, she killed all of them. And for long enough to make it a legend. This woman is evil.

"Don't go!" She begs as the maiden turns around. "You can't leave me. I set you free! I love you!"

"You are deranged."

"Some of the things I have said to you or done to you have been sincere and some have been motive driven. I've danced between both and now everything I do is done out of genuine care and sincere intentions. We need each other."

The maiden cannot hear anymore or she will break either him, the witch, or herself. So she turns and runs out of the pyramid, into the frosted night. Her breath hanging in the air is her only company as she dashes past the house empty handed and is swallowed by the dark forest, looking back to be sure she isn't followed.

With one long look at the witch, the bloke makes up his mind. He crosses the floor and tunes her out as she begs breathlessly to him from the bed. He has one thing he wants to take with him and it smells of honey nectar and is hopefully still in the sick room. As he leaves the cottage with the maiden's journal tucked under his arm, he can still hear the witch pleading.

"We are getting to the point where we understand creation! We are reaching the moment where we understand creation! We are doing what needs to be done! We are creating an alliance! We support each other! We are the evolution! We are the connection! We are the…" And her voice fades out.

Courtney Barriger

The Composer

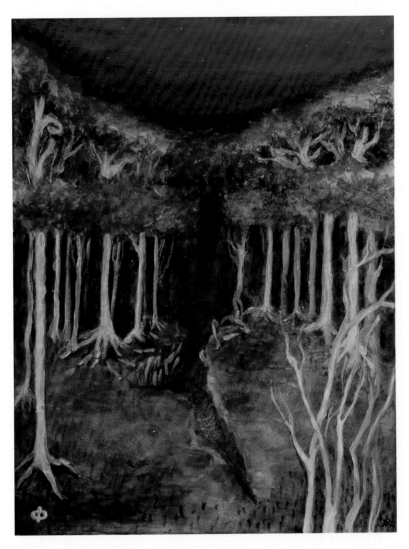

The sky begins to fade out and my eyes grow heavy. My body feels light as air, smooth as water. In the quiet, I take the plunge into the pool of the dream world. The cold swirling depths strip my senses of perception. It sweeps me into a whirling vortex of cushioned liquid. I spin around, a mass of color, unhindered with no place to touch ground. Swaths of black pulse beneath pressured eyelids, quick, faint flashes of light that make my body twitch and writhe, and still, a sense of purity bathes me in frigid waves until my body curls into a ball and holds itself to feel whole again. Heartbeat moves in great swells, warmth spreads to every limb and I unfold again with grace.

Through the pulsing, lucid water, a new vibration is picked up. It tingles the fine hairs in my ears, sending new pulses down my body. The melody agrees with me. It sounds like a crystal glass singing; so natural, so harmonious. Something in it says *listen with your heart and you hear everything.*

The gentle progression of chords breaks the bubble of my sleep and I rise in mystified confusion. The sun has dipped out of the opening in the canopy leaving me in the shade again. I nod my head to the side as if my ears will leak water and once again they pick up a twanging note. The song is real! I listen harder - the melody falls then rises, calling me to my feet. I forget my stubbed toes and am drawn to the edge of the clearing.

But wait! This beautiful song is being played by a person! My eyes flash at the realization. I am not alone after all! Someone else is traveling through the old forest. Whoever it is must be crazy to call attention to them such in a dangerous place. A silly smile drifts across my face. I must meet this musician. There is something about this song and this place…

In a foggy haze I follow the music to the Northern edge of the clearing and duck my head to enter the wild again. The jungle seems easier to pass through; there aren't as many shrubs to beat down and the brambles aren't holding me back any longer. It is growing darker as the sun shares parting words with this side of the planet. Still, the sweet ditty leads me further. As I round the next tree, the wood opens up.

Above, massive branches crisscross over and around each other creating a roof of leaves and twigs. My heart is light and I skip over the fallen leaves on the floor to the beat of the music, the harmony is growing. I am struck with overwhelming urgency to reach the composer before it is finished. I run without comprehension, up and down the leaf-covered slopes, between trunks, knowing nothing but the moving sound of the strings. Don't end, please don't end - I am so close!

As the smooth hill dips down I build momentum and charge up the next slope with double the speed. Zooming into a patch of cherry trees, I direct my concentration to the sight of a huge rotting log in my way, and like a fearless cat, I bound up on top of it and lunge full speed ahead into the air.

"Aaaaaaahhhhh!" The ground suddenly drops. My guts jump into my ribcage and I lose all control in a blinding free fall into darkness. Wind whooshes around and spins in all directions. The lights above dim further and I hit something soft, bounce into the air, and land again dizzy and confused.

What is this! I find myself unable to move. I gasp. In the dim light I discern a sticky rope, as thick as my arm, binding it in place. Grunting, I struggle to free my bonded limb but jump in shock as I realize that my entire body is dangling on a patchwork of ropes. With a heave I yank my right arm from the string and pull my head up to get a look around. It appears that I have fallen into some kind of chasm; a dead forest creek or an abysmal crack in the earth old and forgotten. It is too dark to see the bottom, but in the dim light above I can make out the two dirt walls covered in roots climbing all the way to the surface.

As I sit up and begin to untangle, my ears prick up again. The twanging low-pitched melody resounds up the walls from somewhere not far below. What? This cannot be. The music that was once beautiful and inviting now sounds startlingly ominous; playing louder and louder, rising higher and higher in pitch. Fear floods my mouth and I quickly pull up with all my might to loosen my legs. But these strings are so sticky, too sticky for me to free my entire body at once; I struggle and shake to no avail. And that is when I see it.

Only a few feet down, in the reflection of the parting sun, I see the gleam of different-sized threads, much like the ones I am suspended in, stretched in rows from root to root. And there, perched in a web of his own, sits the great composer himself; climbing the chords of his favorite number on eight sturdy legs. His grotesque body swings and dances, consumed in writing his haunting melody which has, over the years, served to lure the tastiest specimens into his trap.

My vocal chords constrict and a muffled scream escapes my lips, but he doesn't seem to notice me yet. With trembling fingers I frantically work to untie my hair from the web. I breathe as silent as a trespasser as the strands pull free. As I slowly sit up and look desperately for an escape route, my weight teeters on the thread and before I can stop it from happening, my great-grandmother's journal slips from the opening in my book bag and falls, pages flapping in the air and clunks the concentrating composer on the head.

Brilliant, black eyes hit me, eight of them. Like the negative ends of two magnets touching I jump out of my skin into space, too choked to scream. Those eyes tell years of lonely malice built in thick layered webs; of shriveled black carcasses left dangling to rot as the unsatisfying blood of the weak and wretched grows cold in the heart. Those eyes caught off guard and unprotected in a moment of surprise channel a shocking timeline of the wasteful consumption of flesh into my stammering brain.

Then he sees me as I am; a unique, tasty meal, an unchallenged delicacy, a main course that validates the season's stinking leftovers. What a prize! He shakes his rainbow colored abdomen with excitement and climbs higher to survey his dinner. From below he judges the thickness of my thighs and calculates the flavor of my flesh by comparing it to other meals he has had. My skin is rosy and unblemished; he can tell that I have been raised on a healthy diet. With self-control and careful precision he can keep me alive for weeks to enjoy my young, untarnished blood. A small bite here, a small bite there; must not get carried away; it can be made to last.

One-by-one his black arachnid legs hook around the edge of the net; my body flings up and down and I scream, filling the canyon with desperate echoes still unable to move. I watch in horror as my composer extends himself above me, blocking the last light of the day. He takes one final look at his catch and swoops down toward my neck with his mouth open.

The sight of those fangs wakes me up. A shock of adrenaline zaps my system and I lunge the top half of my body out off of the web. Before the drinker knows where the tap went, I snap my jaw around the closest leg, grinding my teeth into crunchy, bitter flesh.

"REEEEEEEE!!!!!" A hiss of pain and anger escapes his gaping mouth. He whips around and quicker than I can follow - BAM! A blow to the chest knocks me back down, blending his eyes into sixteen microscopes. Pulsing eyes of the devil! I am not your dinner! I spit red in his hovering face. "AHHHHH! GET AWAY!"

Still reeling, I notice that I am only held to the web by my sweater and I've landed on a small tear in the fabric.

It is thin, but wide enough for the mind to work through. The web bobs as the composer refocuses. One-by-one, eight bony legs curl around me - a lover's embrace - but before they can pin me down, I know what to do.

In a swoosh I slip through the tear leaving my sweater behind. The composer screams. I fall. My fingers grasp at nothing but stale air that zips by in a hot breath. Then they close around a thick, spiny root. I slam into the canyon wall gasping for breath. The rock is slippery and it is nearly impossible to find footing. I hold on with all of my strength.

But the composer is descending fast. He slinks down the opposite side of the canyon, screening the dark with his bloody eyes. The silence is thick and I hold my breath again. I am shielded from view by a patchwork of hanging roots, but they will not conceal me for long.

If he can't see his prey, he will feel it out. He stretches his long legs flat and slowly creeps across the wall, picking at anything he can reach. A few rocks fly off and tumble into the pit. The horror of his vastness sends shivers down my spine. He knows I am close by. He will see me soon. He will find me soon.

With eyes shut tight I breathe in courage. The roots appear to extend up to the mouth of the canyon. He is scanning the pit below for movement. Breathe.

In a blink I bound up the rock and hoist myself into the roots. Hand-over-hand I move as quickly as I can. There is a maze of string supporting the bulk of the web that is hard to make out in the darkness.

My face is sweating already. I hold my breath again and fold my body to duck through a triangle. The roots extend on both sides of the support string. Swinging my feet to the right, I make it around a high rope and scoot my body through another opening. I wipe my brow. Up five feet is a glimpse of the starry sky. That must be the tear I fell through, it has widened up to the rock face.

A hiss rattles the lower ropes. He knows where I am! My hands begin to shake as I pull myself over the gap and onto loose stone. The roots are thicker, easier to grip but the rocks are dry and crumble at the touch. A root snaps and dirt flies everywhere, sticking to sweat beads and stinging my eyes.

Notes twang up the canyon when he climbs onto the strings. It is a song for my funeral procession. Through the hole in the web those eight empty eyes shine. The composer slides through the tear and onto the rocks.

I hold onto the roots only a few yards from the opening in the chasm but he is closing the gap quickly. A jet of string flies overhead and sticks to the trunk of the cherry tree. The composer latches on. I am two feet from the top, I grasp the edge and hoist myself onto solid ground. He is flying up the rope only a few feet below. I have only seconds to spare.

In desperation I seize the largest rock I see. His hissing face lunges out of the chasm and I heave the stone over my shoulders.

His eyes blink once in surprise before they are knocked in. A pitiful screech fills the canyon and he falls backward bringing loose rubble with him.

Tears flood my eyes but I hold them back. My knees give out and I crumple to the ground.

The woods seem to listen to my breath. My chest rises and falls, the wound leaking blood down my front, and I gather enough strength to scoot to the edge of the chasm.

Resting in his own web is the great composer. The web is torn even more from the rock shower. But the composer himself just looks stunned. His legs are folded over his abdominals, but his hissing breath is still audible.

He is still alive. And so am I.

For a moment I rest, but I know that my bones have to move again. I am so tired, but I must keep going. Tears make mud on my face and I drag myself up off of the dirt. Everything looks the same in all directions; total blackness. How do I read which way I am supposed to take?

This is a nightmare.

Courtney Barriger

The Process of Forgetting

The air buzzes with electricity. For an instant, the murky field is lit as if a mischievous stagehand flicked the floodlights of an empty theater on and off - just to see what the expanse would look like alone without supervision. The blades of grass are heavy with water and shine white in the light as they are beaten down with sheets of freezing rain. They knock around in the breeze but hold tight to their roots as the current dips through their huddled masses, sweeping down the hill like a million swooping snakes to rattle the branches of the lone douglas fir tree at the center of the valley. Then, as quick as it appeared, the lighting is gone and is followed by a thick CRACK BOOM!

All is pitch black again - swirling, impenetrable, mindless black.

This could be the storm of the century for the old, cracked fir tree. In its long-standing life it has taken many thrashings from the whirling symmetrical storms each passing season. Four hundred years the tree has stood its ground. As it began to understand the threatening whispers of the wind, it learned when to tighten its hold to the ground in preparation for the storm. But tonight, the wind no longer whispers but screams out its need for destruction.

In a hissing screech the grass is torn from its roots and joins the flying madness as shredded confetti in the sky. The fir must bow with respect to the storm; its strong limbs bent high up and over in the air to surrender its strength to the more powerful force of nature. In the frenzied blackness, the world seems to give itself away to insanity.

Up the slope of the hill, the wind begins to change direction. Small dead twigs and needles briskly snap off of the branches of the fir and are sucked up into the darkness toward a magnetic force that is forming as a cylinder from the clouds. The heavy branches of the fir bend in on themselves and snap clean in two. Old crusty layers of bark are sucked off to reveal sappy flesh. Dead, rotten chunks of wood attached to living tissue are torn from its trunk. It is stripped clean of decaying impurities and parasitic growth and looks younger than it has for decades. Yet if a tree could scream out in pain, this fir would be hoarse from collapsing its lungs again and again. It holds tight to the ground, as the wind tears at its skin, ripping into living tissue and mindlessly tossing its body like a worn out cat toy.

Beneath its naked surface, shielded from the struggles against the monstrous storm, are countless thin ringlets of bark that loop one after the next out from the vertical heart. Each loop is a year of growth. And every year the heart will bear a fresh new loop to replace the elder loop as its life provider. The very oldest and most experienced of these - the loops who remember the last miniature ice age - live on the farthest, knottiest ends of the fir and do their part to protect the younger layers. New loops are added each year; they do not know the world as well and are still simple and smooth in composition. And at the age of four hundred, the fir tree has grown into a massive mega flora with centuries of stories hidden in these loops beneath many layers of protective bark.

But the storm has already stripped away some of this protection.

Frozen chunks of ice pelt the white, naked outer layer, knocking the tight strips of wood loose. Four hundred-year-old debris flies apart, taking with it the tree's oldest engraved memories; withered, rotten recollections that were tainted from overexposure are now gone: vanished into the darkness.

The cylindrical force moves closer, and the gale is stronger than ever. It tugs and pulls at the weight of the remaining branches, sucking a decade's worth of expanded growth into one chaotic direction. The heavy boughs - worth several lifetimes of careful development, which once supported every extension of the tree's life - scrape and knock into each other in the twisting wind. Once brothers, now enemies, they struggle to remain attached to the trunk at any cost. The fir is bent at a full bow and with an unmerciful CRACK, the trunk snaps in two and the network of branches is sucked into the wind, gone forever.

In the churning haze of the rain, the stump still stands with its roots holding fast to the clay. It has no choice but to rely completely on the strength of its underground life support as the biting wind eats away layer after layer of wood.

The fir is now three-hundred-years-old, and with another hail-filled gust, it is now two-hundred-fifty. It becomes lighter in weight as each exposed memory is taken up into the blackness. Vague swirling years disappear - patterns are stripped away before their existence can even be missed. At one-hundred-years-old the fir admits this is indeed the storm of the century; but then swiftly disregards the thought when another layer is torn away.

For several agonizing hours this continues. The fir becomes lighter and lighter, simpler and simpler with each strip. It does not know its location on the hill and can't recall what type of seed it came from (was it a spore, a seed, a cone?). It does not even remember what type of tree it is. All it knows is the pressure of the wind and the impenetrable blackness of the storm.

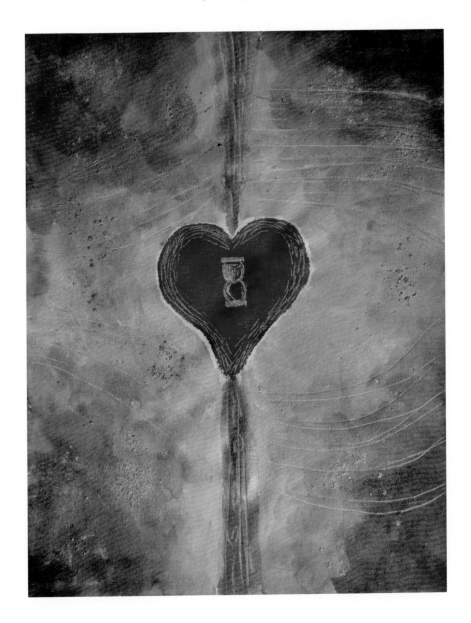

After what could have been a lifetime, the tapering ends of the swirling clouds finally drift over the far edges of the wood. Distant stars pop up here and there, and a shy moon peaks out to greet what is left of the valley.

Standing in the center of the clearing is a fresh, white douglas fir shoot made of only a heart and one infant loop - just enough for it to survive and grow from. The still night is the first thing the fir has ever known. It meets the silence the first time with innocent curiosity and begins recording this peaceful moment in its first ring.

The storm is completely forgotten.

Courtney Barriger

Lady Labyrinth

Everything looks the same in all directions; total blackness. How do I read which way I am supposed to take?

This is a nightmare.

Spiny branches whip by me in a fury as I flee, ripping strings of long, orange hair from my head to be left dangling as confetti in the bristles behind me. A memory of the soft, carpeted drawing room at the homestead torments my stinging agony in flight. And before I can find comfort there, the vision is stripped bare, and every sense of sight and direction is swallowed by this tar black reverie. I tumble blindly, head spinning, tripping and falling over my own feet, in a struggle to grasp anything I can - a tree trunk, a vine – anything that may give way for me to pass.

Speed is my only friend. My will to make it has made an alliance with the time it takes to get there; all time has to do is divide the distance, and quickly. Funny though, this blind terror has propelled me over vast distances so fast, I have lost calculation of time. Thank you loyal speed, but where am I?

The void stretches on and on; a pitch black that masks the swaying mob of jungle pressing in. This conundrum has no end! Trembling hands outstretched, space is a blank mystery to its core, giving no hint of what lay in store. When could I last see? Was that an hour ago or was it five days ago? I blink my eyes, rub them with a fist, and look up where I know the moon once lit the forest floor.

As I break through a low-hanging branch, a jaunty melody prickles my memory. The recollection causes a face spasm. I forget to breath. No, I remember what I last saw. His cunning song still sounds through the far chambers of my mind: a song for me alone. It was so fulfilling, illuminating new passageways with so many resounding chords that only a master could produce; and only an eight-legged monster could perform. I left him unconscious forever ago. He left me blind from shock and with a gaping tear in my chest that strips away any stance that came prior to the attack.

There is something else missing, something that should be on my shoulders. Oh no, the book bag! It fell into the chasm where the freak is sleeping. The bag had provisions, a compass, a machete, and - OH NO! The bag isn't the only thing that fell. My stomach tightens. My great-grandmother's famous journal is what woke the beast from his song! I whip around, the rustling leaves quieting before what was just passed can be sought out again. I grope around to feel for something familiar; a sequence of tree trunks, or a distinctive limb. Everything feels the same. Damn this old forest! There is no way to plot this murky maze, no way to estimate to and fro. It is no wonder I am so lost. I lost my sole motivation for this journey in one moment.

Huffing out hopelessness, the dark is seeping into my ears and entering my mind like a bad smell. Oh, my family will hate me, if they don't already; running off in the middle of the night as a self-righteous pilgrim. I am a thief. The stolen journal was a family heir loom! This slip will never be left to rest. Her comforting voice will never speak to me again through the faded pages of a hero's musings. It takes all of my will to turn my back on that literary spirit guide, but I have no choice. Heart sinking, I crunch onward into a new blind.

Tears stream down my muddy face unguarded. These eyes dried out since the last moments with the composer; their re-acquaintance is met with a sober awareness of how foolish this misadventure has become. I want to scream out, punch a tree, or tear out my hair. Good God, how do I get out of this!

The creaking wood closes in and I shove a small tree aside, sniffing up water that threatens to drip off of my nose, the ground sloping down steeply, I carelessly wipe the drip, and my foot catches on a rock. With a yelp I fly forward, crashing awkwardly through a prickle bush. The floor drops, head first, ink swirls around me as I tumble down natural steps and gain momentum, bumping every corner of my body until stars are bashed into view. Then the ink tilts sideways and my face thuds into the rocky soil.

For a moment I lay in a heap, my ache my only awareness aside from the sharp smells of dewy earth. My chest heaves to catch air that will not enter my lungs. I turn onto my back and stare at the drifting bulbs of light making their way across my universe. And as air floods in I am instantly light headed. I push myself up and press my head with my right hand. With groping hands I move to touch the obstacle that just knocked my head into space. It feels like a gigantic tree trunk the size of a shed, covered in shedding cork-like bark; like a douglass fir tree.

Damned darkness. My shoulder burns, stinging my eyes and I feel something thicker than sweat trickle down my face. The pressure in my head is throbbing. What was that that hit me again? How did I come to be next to a tree? Is this darkness hiding what I think it is - the smell of rotting logs and earth mixed with green growth - is this a forest? What just happened? Feeling the grimy gash on my chest, I wonder how I got it.

Questions aside, the pain is overwhelming, but I force it into a tiny ball and hide it somewhere in my gut, somewhere out of reach. Black! Why is everything dark! I am too tired to be afraid now; I am not even sure why I should be afraid. But that pesky emotion is becoming something else. Where did I just come from? How do I get out? Do I go up the hill? Do I go down? Where will this lead? Where am I? And the moment the pain settles in that hidden place, a swoon threatens to drop me. No matter, I breathe in, I must go on.

But before I can move, the most pleasant sensation flits over my eyes. I am drifting away in my skin, and the little dazzling lights sparkling everywhere have more substance than the tree itself. I blink but they stay with me. Stumbling on, I take a sharp left that feels right. Hands in front, the ground flattens out and the trees open up, and I feel out what seems to be a passage. It is wide enough for me to pass with arms open. Trees make living walls, filling the pathway with a sappy odor. I sneeze halfway through, then the blackness starts to swirl, and I fall.

Weariness hits me in a thick cloud. I slump into a heap in the passage, and I reach for my chest to protect it, coating my hand in sticky, congealed blood. It has stopped bleeding and the wound is numb, but these pulsing stars are making it hard for me to tell if I am recovering or if I am going to pass out.

Gasping, I plant my feet and stand. A gust of air from the left suggests another pathway, but I choose to keep straight. The open forest path curves in and to the right, opening up to what feels like rock and cliff. The space must be gigantic; both deep but somehow endlessly expansive, as if God grabbed the fabric of space and pulled it like pulling a crease in a sheet, far in one direction. Out there is something worth knowing. I hobble to the edge of the rock and try to feel what it could be. A breeze drafts up from the depths below, and a hint of salt in the air stirs some unconscious urge in me. Down, the right way to go is down.

Blindly I descend; boulder, rock, groove and crack, some an even-plane, some so steep I have to climb back up to find a new route. With exactitude and care, the echoes between stones tell how cavernous the fissure is, and the whistle in the wind tells how significant the plunge is. On a jutting boulder that is heavily exposed to the air stream I notice I can see the faintest form of my hands gripping at face rock.

Sight! In an urgency to see what my wounds look like, my weight teeters. I stabilize myself and my curiosity is quelled by the need for safety. With every glance I afford, my pitiful state is more revealed. Instead, I look out to see how the world appears. Off in the distance is the darkest of blues, a deep indigo that stretches the horizontal line in the far expanse. It must be midnight, yet something far away illuminates the indigo in a lighter shade. What could it be? I should know what it is, but I cannot recall it.

Instead of dwelling on this memory lapse, I find a groove and extend my feet down, dangling in space with my toes reaching for a hold, until the pad of my left foot hooks a platform. One after the other, soon I find myself at the bottom of the rocky cliff in the mouth of a canyon. Downward, a faint path snakes through the soaring trees that border the rock wall. Farther on, the path becomes brighter as it tapers away at a curve. I am compelled forward. The trunks are a pale iridescent white against the black shadows, and as I cross the path, I see the slight glow of what must be the source of the light. Everything is in the shine of a small town grown on the edge of an ocean shore.

Get me there now! The path is clear and steady. Over rock and loose soil I shift around boulders. And down, down, I descend, the path leveling out to an even, open wood. Ahead, swathed in a light mist, a towering wall juts out of the canopy, securing the wild outside of the town borders. The air is clearing, and I breathe deeply, enlarging my lungs. When I chance a glance down I see I am coated everywhere in layers of caked dirt and stinking blood, my arms are lacerated and the wounds on my chest are deep. My head is sinking in exhaustion but my destination is so close. I force my feet to walk, force this body to hold it together as I leave the forest behind and cross the threshold of the city.

Through a small open gate in the stone wall, a silent multitude of tall brick buildings are puzzled together in a colorful Tetris that leans down into the ocean. Some of the windows yawn dim lights, as their occupants prepare for bed. Gingerly, I trespass past them, wishing them not to see me like this. They will think I am a beggar. But then again, how do I know I am not?

The cobblestone road almost immediately splits into two paths at the corner of a triangular building. I go right and pass a row of residents till I come to a stone archway. Going under, it gives way to a dusty marble public square. Every door is closed and locked away: nothing to eat, no one to help. In the center, I am disappointed to find there are four ways out of the empty courtyard, all of which look the same. The archway across from the one I entered is a safe a bet as any, so I hobble across; the clink of my steel-toed boots echoing back. I come out into a second courtyard with the same design. *This is a boring look for a city*, I think. Even in pain, my stomach growls.

Through the left archway I find a five-point intersection with a bronze statue of a fisherman casting a net in the center. The surrounding buildings are three-story, some even higher, with brightly painted facades and plant-adorned decks. As pretty as I find these, my feet are dragging and I resolve to curl up in the corner of a nice front porch when I hear voices coming from somewhere off to the right.

I turn right and face a collection of people perched on a staircase outside a turquoise facade. In their early twenties, they are drinking beverages and laughing amongst themselves. They quiet their conversation and stare at me as I hobble up. Their open gawk is unsettling and despite my weariness, I feel a pang of anger.

I know nothing about these people, and their lives are a mystery, but I hate them. Do I hate them because I will never in seven billion years know their thoughts, their history? I only have the one I make up for them now. Now they are a wall of judges, analyzing my state of dress and hair. Can't they see I am wounded? I feel their dislike of me. Do they hate me because they don't know me, or do they hate me because they know exactly what I am made of; the vanity that has me cowering, embarrassed of my weakness. Should I care what they think at all? I am jealous of their contentment. They have contempt for my reckless bravado. The energy of their perceived thoughts weighs me down more than my tired body.

Is this where I am supposed to be? I remember I once had a destination. Was this it, a street full of judges? Down the way to the left there is a fish market; to the right is a narrow street. But what does it matter? I have no place here. No direction will make any of this better.

I am falling again, onto pavement this time. Damn this world. Damn the people who drove me to be here. Damn myself for allowing this. When a person catches me, my vision is gone again and I know it is woman by her soft voice. She says it will be okay and that I am safe.

I am too weak to decline when they take me away. When they slap my face to try to rouse me, I feel a dull thud and hear it seconds later. My hearing must be going too. They place me in what must be a bed in one of their houses. I settle in, calming the urge to lash out into the darkness, only to obey it and tear at anything that comes within reach. Within seconds my arms are banded to my sides. Then my eyes cross and a downward spiraling staircase opens in my imprisoned sight and I fall in head first.

Somewhere above someone asks me my name. At the bottom of the stair is a corridor with row after row of open doors. Yet as I reach them, the doors that stood open for so long, asking for my entrance, close. I try to open one but it is shut tight and nothing comes to me. Forcing a new passage to materialize is futile. I don't remember my name. I think I gave it to someone. Or did they give me theirs?

They ask me where I came from. A door opens up

on its own accord and reveals a room filled with stacks of personal journals, none of which belong to me. A sharp pain stings just below my gut and I remember I am a thief. The floor in the room gives and the journals fall into a chasm. I am in pitch black again and afraid.

Then a new corridor materializes. This one has no doors. Instead, it branches off into other hallways that branch off into other hallways that branch off into other hallways that branch off into other hallways. I turn corners at random, but everything looks the same. I could be going in circles and would never know the difference. Where does any of this lead? If I could split ten ways I could maybe find something at the end of each passage way that presents itself. But as it is just me, which way will take me to the end? Which way do I choose?

Does the fact that I can make choices make me God; that I can go down one path or the other? I remember knowing once upon a time how it felt to be God-like. But how can I be God when I didn't create the corridors? They are just available for my choosing.

But what if I *can* create the corridors? The blue wall to my right is rigid, and I try to turn it into something, anything other than what it is. I imagine a brick wall, a cliff wall, but it stays the same plain blue. As I am trying to force it into a glass wall, the smallest change of color undulates across the surface. I back away.

The blue suddenly has depth even as the wall remains, and far off into it a translucent shimmering something swims in a kaleidoscope of color. I am transfixed. It comes closer and materializes as a near reflection of me; only I am perfectly healed and have a dazzling tail. My face is surrounded by a cloud of my red/orange hair and I look happy. I reach to touch the surface of the glass and so does she. As our hands touch, the glass turns into solid blue and I am alone within the corridors again. But no matter; now I know I can create.

One day the world above opens up to me again and I see an older brown-haired woman with kind eyes smiling down at me. She doesn't speak at first, only sets down a cup of soup on a night stand. Then she tells me that I am allowed to eat if I promise to behave. I don't know what she means until she is untying my restraints and I see a scratch on the side of her neck. I did that?

After the meal an older man with oval glasses and a small notebook comes in, presents himself as the local physician, and asks me a few questions. No I do not remember who I am or were I came from. No I do not remember what happened to me. There was this tree, I think. As he stands in the doorway to leave, he whispers something to the old woman about post-traumatic-stress. I blink rapidly, but cannot recall the trauma that made me this way.

I watch the sun pass over the port town through a small window over my bed. They dressed me in a long white gown that must belong to the old woman, and my wounds are bandaged and have healed significantly while asleep in the coma. I occupy a small spare bedroom with white walls and a red ceiling decorated with promenading zebras located on the bottom floor of a cerulean blue house.

On the cooler days, they help me out to the quaint rose garden in the sandy backyard. I sit and watch the squirrels play only long enough to catch some vitamin D. The healing is slow because of how much blood I need to regenerate. I drink the local yom coconuts as part of a daily regimen. So far it hasn't cleared these annoying white spots from my vision.

According to the doctor, who comes to visit every evening, it is not unusual to slip into fantasy while in a catatonic state. Many of his patients have revisited the events leading up to their traumatic experience in hallucinations of grandeur. It is reassuring to know I am not alone, yet these fantasies are all I have to link me to my history. I visit the corridor every night and meet my past in the most baffling ways.

One evening in the rose garden, as I am staring at the sky trying to determine which bright spot is the sun, the old woman comes out of the house and places a chair directly in front of mine, sitting down to face me with a contemplative expression. This is very direct for her character, so I blink hard to see as much of her as I can.

She begins by telling me that I talk in my sleep. Her room is on the floor above mine, but I cry out loud enough for her to clearly hear what I repeat. Journal, I repeat the word journal over and over in my reverie. I admit that I do dream about journals often and I have told the doctor about it, knowing not what it means. He didn't find it to be anymore substantial than my other fantasies.

The old woman, on the other hand, takes the word more seriously. Fixing me in her compassionate gaze, she insists that it is in the way I say it – the desperation in my voice – that makes it the most genuine thing that has come out of me. The strength in that word is the reason she went to the market today and bought me a gift she swears will change my life. On the deck table, she places before me a very small brown leather-bound journal.

I am speechless at her intensity. When I do not move she takes the book and places it directly into my hands. At the touch of the soft leather a slight confidence rises inside. Without any instruction, she heads back inside, leaving me to ponder how to use this new tool.

That night as I wander the chambers of the blue labyrinth, a beautiful song begins to soak through my soul. I float down a hallway and at a left turn I meet a man in a red and yellow jester suit. As I come closer to him, he smiles and vanishes.

Upon awaking I immediately turn to my bed stand

and grab the journal and a pen. Before he completely leaves me, without hesitation I take that jester and throw him into a wild story that comes up as naturally as exhaling toxic carbon dioxide. After I finish the story, I breathe lighter.

The days pass this way. The NightBook, as I call it, is filled with story after story. The doctor is impressed with the quality of the tales, but unfortunately he does not see credence in them. I however am very pleased with the NightBook and how I have been able to capture the unraveling labyrinth in detail. I come to love the familiar corridors and images my mind plays back. When I close my eyes at night, the pathway is sometimes flanked by trees, and on either side a door will open, showing me a glimpse of what my life looked like in metaphor before I forgot it. As soon as I wake from slumber, I take that pen and record what I can stitch together.

I start to spend my waking hours, which are becoming more vivid daily, writing in the NightBook in the front room; perfecting the style as I read works by other writers from the old woman's bookshelf. Books of poetry inspire me to write poems myself. I jot down an attempt on a blank page in scrawling black ink:

Silent space, a beating heart
zebras prancing overhead
sinking now as images
play above a sandy bed

They float from words on paper
resting on a shelf.
Combined minds of other dreamers
plunge into herself.

Fancies, horrors, laughs and notions
none of which the sleeper made

will merge into her being;
The minds of others, eternal play

And as the sleeper dreams their dreams
drifting through the night
She is what she reads
and you are what I write.

Closing the journal once it is written, I lean back and sink into the cushion. As I exhale, the ache below my gut breaks apart and a light feeling of wellbeing dances over my body. I am surprised and glance down. When I notice the scabs on my arms have crumbled away and my chest now bares a shinny scar, it hits me how much time has passed in healing.

With the NightBook in hand, I return to my room. Finding the most functional outfit gifted to me, I dress in slacks and a button-down shirt and throw on my steel-toed boots. After making the bed, I toss a coat over my shoulder and scavenge the front room for a spare piece of paper. When I can't find one I tear one from the Nightbook and write the old woman a special letter of thanks. Her kindness has truly changed my life.

Out in the city, my instinct guides me down a maze of streets. The sun is high at midday, the air salinity grows stronger and as I turn a corner I see the blue ocean ahead. Down a hill flanked by uniquely designed houses, the steep pavement gives way to a perpendicular boardwalk. The clearness of the day has me skipping along the planks, a cool wind tossing my red hair over my face; I tuck it behind my ears and gaze out at the shimmering ocean. A smile forms on my chapped lips, stretching muscles that have been asleep for weeks. I squeeze them into a fish face to loosen them. Ah, it is beautiful outside.

All along the sunny stretches, flocks of seagulls and

cranes do a dance as they peck up scattered bits of food. I greet the seagulls with a speedy charge and they fly apart, calling angrily at me; but I don't care. The sun kisses my sore skin and a hidden want begins to surface again.

I want ice cream. To the left a ways is where the crowds are, so I stride off in that direction. People pass by. I pass by people. All around are little candy carts and churro heaters. I trade a poem for a chocolate ice cream cone with a young boy who wants to impress his girlfriend. With the coolness going down into my belly, I stand taller and can stand the heat better while I explore.

The boardwalk holds an eclectic group of transplants to be sure. There are jugglers, hoola-hoopers, magicians, singers, animal trainers, tarot card readers, dancers, merchants, sailors, tourists, couples, children, pets, cranes and seagulls, and countless other types within the masses; each calling louder than the next. Tourists bustle by to catch a good spot before the next act begins. I press through, interested in watching a dog jump through a hoola-hoop. The heat has me sweating so I pull the belt from my coat to make a headband, just like the tarot card reader is wearing. Circling around a crowd that is watching two mimes with fluffy neck-ruffles pretend to ride a tandem bicycle, something catches my eye: something orange.

Leaning against the boardwalk railing is the portrait of a woman with flaming red hair drifting though a black, star studded outer space on stretched canvas. It is startlingly familiar. I push through the crowd in a rush to get a closer look. Past this striking picture is another of a redheaded ballerina dancing on stage with a jester in a red and yellow checkered jumpsuit. I blink my eyes a few times to be sure I am not dreaming. When I search the row I am equally shocked to see other paintings that resemble my labyrinth dreams. At the end of the row, my eyes land on the figure of a white-haired woman who has an apron filled with paint brushes that reads "Peace. Love. Community."

I quickly duck behind a display of rugs next to her setup before she senses my presence. With a maroon shrug shielding me from view, I watch as the painter fiddles with a dream catcher necklace she wears. Then she digs into her apron to find a box of matches and lights a stick of incense that is stuck into a crack in the wood. Once it is going she turns back around and a stranger approaches her.

He asks her something. She appears to give him directions, but there is a strange glint in her eyes. As she leans in close, her hand slips ever so quickly into the stranger's pocket. He thanks her for her guidance and heads off to where she sent him, and she drops his wallet into her paintbrush pocket, looking casual as ever.

Frowning at this action, I still can't help but be curious to meet her. That is until I witness her reaction when a redheaded woman close to my age passes by her display. At first glance she lights up, stepping out from her lean on the handrail. Then a shade of green passes over her face and her posture breaks, making her look disfigured and substantially older. She lets out a low growl and as the strange redhead comes by, she barks obscenities at her until the poor girl rushes away from the abuse.

My chest stings where the wound was. *Hhmm*, I think, *better I not chance a bad retort in my condition.* So as an equestrian leads a horse by the display, I jump at the opportunity to hide behind the giant Clydesdale's flanks. After twenty yards, I hope never to cross paths with that weird white-haired woman again. However she came to possess a mind for dreams like mine; that will be a mystery I hope never to know.

As I think on the paintings, I catch the tail end of a song coming from up ahead. The solo guitar that cuts through the chattering masses has a hauntingly beautiful melody; it fits the space I have below my gut so perfect I might either be sick or it might heal me. I skirt through the crowd carefully to see where it is coming from. There, on the edge of the boardwalk looking down at the rocky shore is a young man in his late twenties with a cherry wood guitar, playing a song that sounds wholly personal.

On the ledge are a few stacked books and articles and one leather bound book that is wound tight with a thin rope. His tenor voice rises and falls, pulling me out of hiding to get a closer look at the man who bares his soul in verse. I listen to the words. This one is an about Eros and a woman who apparently ruined his life.

> I told you you were beautiful;
> Long legs, raven hair to kill.
> But the fire is burnt out,
> You dirty cheap thrill.
> I'll be the first to leave.
> Your voice, so very shrill;
> Will be drowned out
> By these little round pills.

The words destroy the exquisiteness present in the melody. It doesn't suit me, I decide. And as I pass by to continue my little adventure, he catches my eye and winks at me. My heart leaps in my chest unexpectedly. I feel almost provoked to run from the feeling. The stretched scar over my chest hurts as his gaze drifts over my body. I am about to wave back, a simple gesture to acknowledge him in passing, when I turn and see something much more provoking.

A ways down, a three-mast trade ship with the name Indaco painted boldly on the stern in bright blue is docked at the end of the boardwalk. It is teeming with sailors and merchants who move to and fro following orders in a clear cut system that is performed punctually. All of the action on board makes the ship itself look alive! The purpose behind the sailors' actions, their direction is so attractive. My arm drops its salutations and I leave the musician watching me as I go on.

As I approach the Indaco, passing by the last of the performers, I see the young sailors are carrying crates and boxes on board, carting goods up ramps with large ropes and large muscles. They whistle down at me and call me pet names as I reach the side of the giant ship. The tall, lean ramp guard shouts an order for the men to quiet and get back to work. Flicking his straight blond hair back to see who is coming up, he is pleasantly surprised to see me; it shows openly only briefly before he masks it.

The ramp is slick, and when I board my feet slip. I dismiss the hand the young sailor offers and carefully place my feet on the plank until I am level with him. The wind is strong up here, and it flicks my hair behind me. He stands stationary, waiting to know what I want. Some of the other sailors pause to watch the interaction, but with the slightest nod in their direction, they snap back into a semblance of business. Behind the sailor, the indigo bay stretches out into the deep blue waters. He reads something in my wonderment and clears his throat to draw me back.

I take my time to look him over for a moment as I think of what to say, his broad shoulders distracting me while his almond shaped eyes study my face beyond its features. It is a labor to pull breath, and before I know what I am asking, the words tumble over my lips.

"I would like to meet your captain."

The sailor purses his lip and raises his eye brows. He studies me; as a young, strangely disconnected woman with nothing on her but a small bag, I must appear juvenile. What could I want? He seems to find something he is looking for behind my eyes and nods his head; a smirk plays his face as if he finds amusement in the request. Without further examination he turns and heads directly toward the Captain's quarters. I follow behind, unsure if he means for me to.

Inside the cabin, lights dance around the Captain's head when he asks me what good I could be on board a ship of merchant sailors. I am clearly very weak and ill suited for life at work on the sea. But that fight to survive works through me again, and I fight to find the perfect way to approach it. I dig into my bag and hand him the leather bound Nightbook. His eyes scrutinize my intent, but he takes it from me anyway.

Minutes pass and he reads the deepest of my inner struggles, unfolding on paper in metaphor. His eye brows rise, he laughs out loud, his face becomes somber and still, as he pages through. Without finishing he hands it back to me, a calculated look of postulation on his rugged face.

"You have quite the imagination," he grunts.

I have nothing to say to that. No way to explain my motivation without sounding crazy.

"Where do you hail from?"

"Sir, this journal is all I have on my past."

"Interesting," he stares at me like the sailor on deck did.

"But that is an asset!" I exclaim, "Because I have no baggage! All I know is that I can write adventure stories; and a life at sea, what an adventure that must be!"

He snorts at the mild rhyming. I am offended. He doesn't care.

"Well, dear, it will be interesting to see how you manage on the Indaco. We have a shipment due three days north of here. This passage will be your test. And I suggest you try your best." We share a grin. "And start your stories tomorrow, beginning with mine!"

"Thank you Captain," I manage to get out.

"And the First Mate will find out how useful you can be. Where is he?" The Captain leers his head to the side, "Hey!" he barks. The young sailor who escorted me to the Captain's quarters enters at attention. The Captain points to where he wants him to stand and he obliges but a foot from the point.

"Starting your first day strong I see. Well mate number one, show this lady below deck to the former assistant cook's quarters. A single bed in the kitchen on the far side away from the bros should do. She is to try the kitchen first, and if it doesn't suit, try her as a lookout; she is small enough to fit in the barrel atop the mast I believe." I stand from the desk to follow the First Mate and hear the Captain bark one more order. "See to it she gets a pen and notebook asap!"

After I see the cot behind the kitchen where I will be sleeping, I head to the upper deck again before we set berth. The sailors have caught wind that I will be the ship's documentary writer, and most of them are pretty happy about it; high-fiving me and blowing me kisses. I roll my eyes and make my way to the starboard side to say goodbye to the forest, the city, and my deviated mind.

The men bustle to unlink the rope and chain from the dock and heave as they crank up the anchor. Overhead, the masts creak as the giant canvas sails flap open, catching the rushing wind and filling out. The boardwalk drifts by and I wave at the colorful masses and they wave back. The guitar player notices me and waves over.

"Bye, bye my love!" I shout back with no reason.

And the Indaco cuts a circle in the bay and catches the northern trade winds. The upward sloping old forest and far off cliffs disappear around the bend, and as the landscape turns, up ahead are tall, blue mountains; the farthest peaked in white snow. Distinct beaches become a fine yellow line, and then disappear entirely. And soon, the world is only the Indaco and the endless expanse of shimmering water.

At the helm it is all I can do to keep my eyes from watering. The men cannot witness a tear, or I will never gain their respect. So I let the moment settle in my heart and hold the NightBook close to my chest. I don't realize I am humming until I notice I am not alone.

The First Mate stands silently at my right, watching the horizon line and chancing closer looks at me. My hum tapers out slowly and I let the NightBook lower to my side and stand up taller in an attempt to look less girly. He puts out a hand and waits until I understand that he wants to read my journal.

"Not now," I say, watching the sky darken as the sun sets toward where we left the mountains, "that story needs to be put away for a time." His head lifts as he considers my meaning, and he squints at me. Not knowing how else to say it, I sigh;

"I want to be free."

His eyes sparkle and his face opens up. In a short laugh he shakes his head at me, and in merriment he says, "You are free," and leaves me with silent tears streaming down my face. I blink and look out at the ocean noticing the little lights have left my vision. With relief I wipe the tears away with the back of my hand and let the wind clear my face of any redness.

This NightBook can be laid to rest. It is time to toughen up and prepare for the next adventure.

Meet the Author

Steve Nyman

Courtney Barriger is from Jacksonville Florida.
NightBook is her first novel. She now lives in
Los Angeles and continues to pursue her passion
for writing and the arts.

You can find her online at

www.nightbooknovel.com